Love Advice for Women

Love Advice for Women

Everything you wanted to know about love
from Jane Austen to Virginia Woolf

Nathaniel Jackson

ADVICE **ZONE**

Washington, D.C.

AdviceZone books and audio-tapes may be purchased directly either from the AdviceZone website at *www.advicezone.com,* by calling toll-free at 1-800-210-ZONE or faxing the order form on page 143 to (732) 225-1562.

For acknowledgments of the use of artwork, see page 136. For acknowledgments of the use of copyrighted material, see page 137.

Library of Congress Cataloging-in-Publication Data

Jackson, Nathaniel A.
   Love Advice for Women: Everything you wanted to know about love from Jane Austen to Virginia Woolf/Nathaniel Jackson. Includes Index. 1st ed.
ISBN 0-9668725-0-9 (paperback)

1. Love advice 2. Self help 3. Interpersonal Relationships
I. Title
646.7'7-dc20   98-96870

Printed in Hong Kong. Cover design by Bookwrights, Charlottesville, VA., Mayapriya Long. Interior design by Soleil Associates, Washington, D.C., Judith L. Smith.

Cover picture: (detail) *Der Kuss* ("The Kiss") by Gustav Klimt. Reproduced by permission of Österriechische Galerie Belvedere, Vienna, Austria.

DEDICATION

To the memory of Joseph F. Unanue.

Hemingway defined courage as "grace under
pressure." Joe, you had both courage and grace.
We miss you.

ACKNOWLEDGMENTS

No book is created in a vacuum and this compilation is no exception. I give my
heartfelt thanks to the following people for their many contributions:

Shobha Sarah George for all her help and support, but mostly for just being Shobha;
Mayapriya Long, for her classic design of the cover series; Judy Smith, for her creative
design of the book interior; Dan Poynter, for showing me the way; Chris Roerden, for
her countless excellent editing suggestions; Janice Tuten, for her sharp eyes and many
ideas; Donald Cornish, for helping to design the supporting website for the book; Claudia
Ruiz Nava, for helping this whole enterprise take life; Lancelot d'Ursel and Saeko
Tsuchihashi, for believing in the dream; and finally, I'd like to thank my family and friends
for supporting this extended "labor of love."

Love for his wonders in this worldly scene
Confound me so that when I think of him
I scarcely know whether I sink or swim....
Where proof is lacking by some other test,
Believing in old books is best.

Geoffrey Chaucer, *The Birds' Parliament*

CONTENTS

PREFACE

This book was born of necessity. Several years ago, I retreated to the romantic hills of Guanajuato, Mexico, with about two hundred classic novels and plays and the usual yearning of a neophyte writer to create a classic of my own. However, I encountered a roadblock much more formidable than the usual writer's block: I fell under the spell of "fantasy" love. I knew enough to recognize that when one is in this delirious stage, one is not able to "see" things as they really are. Unfortunately, I was without my usual network of friends and family—my quaint quarters lacked a phone—who would normally steer me through the treacherous Scylla and Charybdis of nascent love. Thus, for advice I had to fall back on my stack of readings from Sappho, Ovid, Stendhal, de Beauvoir, and friends. Naturally some of their advice seemed dated, sexist, or just plain wrong. Aristotle, for example, insisted that men who married too soon would stunt their growth. Yet a remarkable amount of advice still rang true: generally the part that pertains to human nature. As for the dynamics between the sexes, which have changed so much over the last generations, I relied on more modern sources.

And so the *Love Advice* series was, almost accidentally, created. Immersed in the literature of love, I gradually realized that annotated anthologies of advice compiled for women and men could help many people as it helped me, especially those of us who temporarily lack a rudder in those difficult periods that we lovers inevitably face. So I sought advice that would succor all those afflicted by the curious ways of love, from the earliest intimations of infatuation through marriage—or, if unfavored by Venus, to the charred ashes of what once was a great passion. Much of the love advice—in addition to being a joy to read—is simple common sense rather than any great revelation. But its simplicity makes this love advice no less valuable; as Samuel Johnson observed, "People need to be reminded more often than they need to be instructed."

Some readers may object that we cannot "manage" our love lives like our finances, although both may be subject to some luck and vicissitudes. True; love is not like a cake that can be made by following a recipe. But even if we cannot create love as a cook creates a cake, this does not mean that advice on loving is useless. Advice on love might not transform any of us into an amazing lover, but it can—through awareness and reflection— prevent some of our more egregious errors and help us to recognize whether we are experiencing genuine love or some transient, ersatz variety. Through a better understanding of love, we can reduce many of the frustrations that arise from some of the contradictory demands we make of love.

Since this is not a scholarly undertaking but rather a collection of quotations on the wisdom and follies of love, the tone of my commentary ranges from theoretical to playful, depending on the subject matter. This is based upon the theory that too much commentary would only get in the way of the fun. My empathy is always with those truly in love, but this does not preclude our laughing at the follies committed in the name of love.

As in any anthology, personal preferences of the editor have eased their way into the selection process, but I tried to collect advice from a wide universe of authors and let the weight of advice speak for itself. I made a sincere effort to cull quotations from women and men writers of many cultures and periods, because a variety of perspectives can offer the most comprehensive outlook. Of course, given the wide range of authors and eras, the resulting advice on love is somewhat varied. Indeed, the conception of love itself has undergone quite a transformation from ancient times to today's so-called "modern" conceptions of love. Even the authors themselves were not consistent in their advice—indeed, they sometimes contradicted themselves, quite dramatically, in different stages of their lives. Therefore as editor I have tried to choose those quotations that I think will be most universal and most helpful for those of us firmly entrenched in the modern era. I would also like to encourage those who have great love advice quotations from other classic books to send them along to our website at *www.advicezone.com/quotes/*. We will gratefully acknowledge any quotations used in subsequent editions or books in the *Love Advice* series.

To put some of the authors' quotations in some context, I have included short love-life biographies throughout the text. (You can read these love-life biographies in greater detail at the book's website *www.advicezone.com/bios/*). From these mini-biographies, you can see that the love lives of these great writers were often as complicated and turbulent as those experienced by the rest of us, if not more so. Rarely do we find a great writer or thinker with a happy, so-called "normal" love life. Perhaps this is because requited happiness in love tends to dull the poet's quill, or if not, to make the writer's literary creations rather dull indeed. But the love woes of these authors may not be in vain; after all, we can still learn from their misfortunes, or to paraphrase Bismarck, "Fools learn from their own mistakes, the wise learn from the mistakes of others."

As for my own foolish mistakes in love, let me confess that I've made my fair share, as most of us mortals do. But on the whole, it's been a fascinating journey and I have very few regrets. My consolation is that I've tried to learn along the way, and the quotations in this book and the forthcoming *Love Advice for Men* have helped keep me from committing even more absurd errors in love. It has been a great joy to compile these quotations—a labor of love, as some have called it—and the process has been both humbling and instructional. St. Augustine puts it better: "I am the sort of man who writes because he has made progress, and who makes progress by writing." My earnest hope is that *Love Advice for Women* will help your own progress in love as well.

hat is this thing called love?

Is love organic or a product of civilization?

Understanding the apparent paradox of love

An "updated" theory of love: fantasy vs. mature love

Love: "The Divine Madness"

What is love, anyway? Is it just one of those things that we can't define, but we know it when we feel it? Certainly the many philosophers who have written about love have not come to any consensus. Plato viewed love as an appreciation of beauty, particularly intellectual beauty. Lady Murasaki Shikibu of tenth-century Japan saw love as a restless yearning, often doomed to meet a tragic ending. Dante viewed love as part of a larger universal focus: "the love that moves the stars." And Freud defined (or perhaps confined) love as an impulse of inhibited or delayed sexuality.

With all this confusion about the very nature of love, perhaps it is futile to even venture a set definition:

So far only one incontestable truth has been stated about love: This is a great mystery; everything else that has been written or said about love is not a solution, but only a

Left: "The Dream," Marc Chagall, 1939

*statement of questions that have remained unanswered. The explanation that would fit
one case does not apply to a dozen others, and the very best thing, to my mind, would
be to explain every case separately without attempting to generalize. Each case should
be individualized, as the doctors say.*   **Anton Chekhov,** *About Love*

So should we give up trying to define what love is? Not necessarily. Pausanias, of
Plato's *Symposium*, believes there are several types of love that can be identified:

*If there were only one Love, then what you said would be well enough; but since there
are more Loves than one, you should have begun by determining which of them was to
be the theme of our praises.*   **Plato,** *Symposium*

Perhaps a better way of approaching a subject so vast and confusing is to begin by
professing that love cannot be confined to a few distinct categories, but instead is a whole
galaxy of emotions and attitudes, existing simultaneously and often in direct contradiction
to each other. My personal favorite definition of love comes from Zora Neale Hurston:

*...love ain't somethin' lak a grindstone dat's de same thing everywhere and do the same
thing tuh everything it touch. Love is lak de sea. It's uh moving thing, but still and all,
it takes its shape from de shore it meets, and it's different with every shore.*
Zora Neale Hurston, *Their Eyes Were Watching God*

Another fascinating aspect of love is that the experiences are so different, even for the two
people involved in a relationship:

*First of all, love is a joint experience between two persons—but the fact that it is a joint
experience does not mean it is a similar experience to the two people involved. There are*

the lover and the beloved, but they come from different countries. Often the beloved is only a stimulus for all of the stored-up love which has lain quiet for a long time hitherto. And somehow every lover knows this....

Now, the beloved can also be of any description. The most outlandish people can be the stimulus for love. A man may be a doddering great-grandfather and still love only a strange girl he saw in the streets of Cheehaw one afternoon two decades past. The preacher may love a fallen woman. The beloved may be treacherous, grease-headed, and given to evil habits. Yes, and the lover may see this as clearly as anyone else—but that does not affect the evolution of his love one whit. A most mediocre person can be the object of a love that is wild, extravagant and beautiful as the poison lilies of the swamp. A good man may be the stimulus for a love both violent and debased, or a jabbering madman may bring about in the soul of someone a tender and simple idyll. Therefore, the value and quality of any love is determined by the lover himself.

Carson McCullers, *The Ballad of the Sad Café*

Part of our difficulties in defining love result from the fact that the word "love" in English encompasses a whole range of emotions, from loving our parents to "loving" music or from spiritual love to erotic love. The ancient Greeks eliminated much of this semantic confusion by designating several types of love: *agape* (religious love, love of humanity), *eros* (sexual love), and *philia* (friendship, brotherly love). For now we are concerned only about romantic love, in all its strange and wonderful permutations.

Is love organic or a product of civilization?

The concept of love, it is sometimes argued, is merely a product of civilization, particularly of advanced societies. Even a great romantic such as Stendhal argues that love is confined to the refined classes:

Carson McCullers (1917 – 1967)

Lula Carson Smith, author of The Member of the Wedding *and* The Ballad of the Sad Café *married Reeves McCullers, a fellow Southerner, at the age of twenty. Reeves unfortunately chose to be a writer and felt he had to compete with his more talented wife.*

He never ceased to love his wife, but their marriage wreaked havoc on his emotional life. They divorced in 1941 and remarried in 1945, after Reeves' discharge from the Army.

In 1952, Carson and Reeves bought a home in a village outside Paris. Neither was well at the time: both had been drinking heavily for many years. Carson had attempted suicide in 1948, but that attempt cured her forever of the impulse. Reeves, on the other hand, had become suicidal over his relationship with his wife and his lack of career since leaving the army, and he several times proposed a double suicide to Carson.

Terrified for her life after one such proposal, Carson fled to America, leaving Reeves to kill himself a few weeks later, alone in a Paris hotel. She refused to pay the cost of having his ashes sent to her. Many friends were alienated by her complete refusal to mourn him.

Love is civilization's miracle. Among savages and barbarians only physical love of the coarsest kind exists.

Stendhal, *On Love*

Echoing Stendhal, Friedrich Nietzsche argues that the concept of romantic love was invented by the twelfth-century troubadours of Provence, France:

Love as passion—it is our European specialty—absolutely must be of aristocratic origin: it was, as is well known, invented by the poet-Knights of Provence, those splendid, inventive men of the gai saber *to whom Europe owes so much and indeed, almost itself.*

Friedrich Nietzsche, *Beyond Good and Evil*

But these arguments ignore all the romantic literature that precedes the twelfth century, such as the love poems of Sappho, the romantic novels of Murasaki Shikibu, Arabic love poetry, or the annals of love from India or China. Clearly, romantic love is not only global but also has been around for a very long time; witness the love poetry found on ancient Egyptian papyri and vases dating between 1300 and 1100 B.C. The theory of invented love also seems counter-intuitive, because nobody really teaches us to feel love, we innately feel it. This universality of innateness seems to be backed up by convincing statistics: a recent study conducted by anthropologists William Jankowiak and Edward Fischer found evidence of romantic love in nearly 90 percent of the 166 cultures they studied.

Yet some anthropologists and historians are happy to recite to us that romantic love is a relatively recent invention, a product of privilege and luxury. In other words, where there is no leisure, there is no love:

Love is the invention of a few high cultures, independent, in a sense, of marriage— although society can make it a requisite for marriage, as we periodically

attempt to do. But in terms of a personal, highly intense choice, it is a cultural artifact.
Margaret Mead, quoted in the *New York Times*

As for the leisure argument, while it is true serfs and slaves were not afforded the luxury of an elaborate mating dance, this does not mean that genuine love did not develop between individuals. Even a cursory reading of slave narratives in the *ante bellum* United States such as *Incidents in the Life of a Slave Girl* by Harriet Jacobs shows that powerful and deeply romantic love can develop even among the most deprived of couples.

If the feelings of love are not radically altered by economics, the "game" of love surely is. The twelfth-century aristocratic "love courts" of Provence could deliberate over the fine points of courtly love, but the serfs laboring on their masters' estates had no time for such fine distinctions. Nor was chastity held in an exalted state by the laboring classes. The abiding point is that the capacity to love appears to be innate and *not* cultural, though the rules of the game may differ by society.

What *is* characteristic of the leisure society—from the imperial court of tenth-century Heain Japan to today's sometimes jaded versions—is the nurturing, fantasizing, and packaging of love. These love stories, whether they take the form of novels, plays, or movies, tend to concentrate on the amorous mating games, the period of suspense when the fate of the lovers is not known. Typically, the book or movie ends as the beleaguered lovers, having surmounted every conceivable obstacle, are happily ensconced in each other's arms. Eternal domestic bliss is naturally assumed once the lovers are joined.

But isn't the presumption of bliss inherent at the start of every love match? We all have a tendency to believe that if we "get" the love we desire, all will be well. And yet we know that nearly half of all marriages end in divorce. Tolstoy reminds us of the futility in searching for happiness in obtaining the "other":

...the eternal error men make in believing that happiness consists in the realization of their desires.   **Leo Tolstoy,** *Anna Karenina*

So how is it that love that so often starts out so promising dissolves into something considerably short of bliss? Why does love that seems so good sometimes go bad?

Understanding the apparent paradox of love

It seems absurd that one concept, love, could contain so many paradoxes and contradictions. We know from experience and proverbs that love should be enduring, and yet it is all too often fleeting. Or it should be all seeing, and yet everyone knows that "love is blind." Another seeming paradox of love is the belief that for love to be "exciting," it must be something tumultuous and "stormy":

> *This level reach of blue is not my sea;*
> *Here are sweet waters, pretty in the sun,*
> *Whose quiet ripples meet obediently*
> *A marked and measured line, one after one.*
> *This is no sea of mine, that humbly laves*
> *Untroubled sands, spread glittering and warm.*
> *I have a need of wilder, crueler waves;*
> *They sicken of the calm, who knew the storm.*   **Dorothy Parker,** *"Fair Weather"*

But eventually the tempest abates, and the lover is left with the tiresome calm. How do we reconcile these contradictions?

One explanation is to consider love as a continuum rather than as a single concept with conflicting guises, depending on the whims of Cupid. By a "continuum of love" I mean that the would-be lover often starts with an infatuation based on a few superficial stimuli. I call

Dorothy Parker
(1893 – 1967)

The doyenne of the famous Algonquin Round Table was known primarily for her pithy poetry and witty remarks.

The year Dorothy Parker joined **Vanity Fair** *as a drama critic, she met and married Edwin Pond Parker II. She confessed not long after the wedding that "I married him to change my name" (which was Rothschild) and escape from the "mongrel" past she later said she despised.*

She eventually divorced Mr. Parker, had several unhappy love affairs, and later married an actor-writer named Alan Campbell, who was eleven years younger than she. After a decade of marriage, they divorced, but reconciled after a few years.

this stage "fantasy love." Based on the actions of the lover (and of course, the responses of the beloved), the infatuation can move to a more stable stage, characterized by more realism and, one hopes, more stability. I call this later stage "mature love."

The concepts of "fantasy love" and "mature love" are not necessarily discrete categories, but rather different points along the continuum of loving. Therefore it is not a paradox that a "mature" love can be highly romantic, or a "fantasy" love involve quite genuine feelings of tenderness for the partner. By using this concept of continuum we are able to see that love can take many guises and not be contradictory, though it would be futile to claim that love is consistent!

An "updated" theory of love: fantasy vs. mature love

How can we distinguish between a transient passion and a mature love? Infatuation is a projection of desire, a delightful phantasm, a reflection of our deep need for connection. And since it is a projection, it is not grounded in reality.

On the other hand, mature love can thrive only on the basis of knowledge of the beloved. This is not to imply that it is boring, by any means: a mature love certainly can include romantic love, and indeed thrives on romantic gestures. The distinction between romance and fantasy is that romance is a joy, a recognition, an expansion to include another being. Fantasy love, on the other hand, is a projection based largely on initial impressions and the fanciful flights of heated imagination.

Another distinction between fantasy love and mature love is that the love fantasist creates his or her own deity to worship. Mature lovers see and understand their beloveds for what they are and accept them, warts and all. But mature love is more than just friendship and respect raised to a supernal level; rather it is a deep instinctual pull toward the other:

...what makes true love is not the information conveyed by acquaintance, not any circumstantial charms that may therein be discovered: it is still a deep and dumb affinity, an inexplicable emotion seizing the heart, an influence organizing the world, like a luminous crystal, about one magic point.   **George Santayana,** *The Life of Reason*

Indeed, a mature love is even more than an act of instinct; it is also an act of the soul:

...a centrifugal act of the soul that goes towards the object uniting with it and positively affirming its being.   **José Ortega y Gasset,** *On Love: Aspects of a Single Theme*

Love: "The Divine Madness"

Plato's wonderful expression to define love as "the divine madness" is so affecting because it acknowledges that the strong visceral attachment to the beloved is not particularly rational—and hence a sort of madness. But there is a kind of divinity in our visceral choice of the beloved. While it is true that the lover often constructs an ideal to worship, this doesn't mean that the love is any less valid.

In fact, without this intuitive insight into the "angelic" nature of the beloved, the result can be affection without the divine connection that constitutes love:

Whenever this ideality is absent and a lover sees nothing in his mistress but what everyone else may find in her, loving her honestly in her unvarnished and accidental person, there is a friendly and humorous affection, admirable in itself, but no passion or bewitchment of love; she is a member of his group, not a spirit in his pantheon.

          George Santayana, *The Life of Reason*

One of the messages that Plato imparts is not to be afraid of "spiritual" aspects of love—there is something deep and abiding in these instincts. In fact, the very lack of rationality is one of the most appealing aspects of a great love, which could be defined as:

> *...a secret alliance, with the intention to belong to, and share with each other,*
> *a mystical estate; mystical exactly in the sense that the real experience cannot be*
> *communicated to others, nor even explained to oneself on rational grounds.*
> **Katherine Anne Porter,** *Marriage Is Belonging*

   Although a mature love may not be wholly rational, it doesn't mean we can just lay back and wait for mature love to overcome us. Aristotle said that love is an activity, and the act of loving was superior to just being loved. If we are to learn more about the various stops along the bumpy continuum of love, we should begin our search with the exhilarating stages of fantasy love.

Being with you or without you is how I measure my time.

—Jorge Luis Borges, The Threatened One

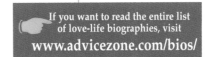

Fantasy love: symptoms and stages

Early symptoms of fantasy love:

> *Feeling shy*
> *Daydreaming*
> *The uniqueness of the beloved*
> *Neglecting food and sleep*

Stages in the birth of fantasy love:

> *Sudden attraction*
> *Hope*
> *Doubts about the beloved*
> *Obstacles*
> *Anxieties and jealousies*
> *Desire for immediate commitment*

Fantasy love is:

> *A reflection of a desire for connection*
> *A projection of our desires*

This is why "love" sometimes seems to be:

> *Blind*
> *An illusion*
> *Folly*
> *Madness*

Left: "Two Women at a Window," Bartolome Murillo, c. 1655/1660

Early symptoms of fantasy love:

Do you think you are falling in love? Are you saying remarkably silly things, day-dreaming when you should be working, and basically ignoring the rest of the world? These are but a few of the telltale signs that you are falling under the spell of fantasy love.

Feeling Shy

The first symptom of incipient love is that your heart starts beating furiously in the presence of the object of your affection:

> *Love is so very timid when 'tis new.*   **Lord Byron,** *Don Juan*

The second symptom is the inability of your tongue to move in its accustomed unfettered fashion in the presence of the adored. Don't worry; you're not stupid. You're just infatuated. My favorite poet of ancient Greece, Sappho, tells us to blame it on the gods of love:

> *Aphrodite, the dictator*
> *of hearts, has made you dumb.*   **Sappho,** *The Love Songs*

The positive development in all this nonsensical behavior is that this very shyness creates a sort of unacknowledged intimacy, as noted by George Eliot in her masterpiece *Middlemarch*:

Lydgate, naturally, never thought of staying long with [Rosamond], yet it seemed that the brief, impersonal conversations they had together were creating that peculiar intimacy which consists in shyness. They were obligated to look at each other in speaking, and somehow the looking could not be carried through as the matter of course which it really was. Lydgate began to feel this sort of consciousness unpleasant, and one day looked down, or anywhere, like an ill-worked puppet. But this turned out badly: the next day Rosamond looked down, and the consequence was, when their eyes met again, both were more conscious than before....

> [T]hat intimacy of mutual embarrassment, in which each feels that the other is feeling
> something, having once existed, its effect is not to be done away with. Talk about the
> weather and other well-bred topics is apt to seem a hollow device, and behavior can hardly
> become easy unless it frankly recognizes a mutual fascination, which of course need not
> mean anything deep or serious.   **George Eliot,** *Middlemarch*

Daydreaming

Mooning about your beloved is the next infallible symptom of falling in love. Or as
Sappho says:

> I'm baffled
> I do not know
> what to do
> my mind's
> in two.   **Sappho,** *The Love Songs*

The slightest comment, the pettiest gesture, becomes a source of intense rumination, not
to mention interpretation:

> Young love-making—that gossamer web! Even the points it clings to—the things whence
> its subtle interlacings are swung—are scarcely perceptible: momentary touches of fingertips,
> meetings of rays from blue and dark orbs, unfinished phrases, lightest changes of cheek
> and lip, faintest tremors. The web itself is made of spontaneous beliefs and indefinable
> joys, yearnings of one life towards another, visions of completeness, indefinite trust.
>
>   **George Eliot,** *Middlemarch*

The uniqueness of the beloved

The next obvious tendency is to construct a reason why the object of your affection is a
unique creature:

*My thoughts
rush headlong;
my words
are confused;
for love does not
recognize order.*

**—St. Jerome,
Epistulae**

**Kate Chopin
(1851 –1904)**

The writer of The Awakening, *which caused a national scandal for its "indecency," was an independent spirit who dressed unconventionally and smoked cigarettes.*

At nineteen, she married Oscar Chopin and promptly had a half-dozen babies during her first decade as a wife.

After her husband's sudden death in 1882, she took over the management of the family plantation in Louisiana.

As a widow, she continued to live an unconventional life, writing short stories for Vogue *and* Atlantic Monthly. *She is generally regarded as America's first woman novelist.*

"If I were young and in love with a man," said Mademoiselle, turning on a stool and pressing her wiry hands between her knees as she looked down at Edna, who sat on the floor holding the letter, "it seems to me he would have to be some grand esprit; *a man with lofty aims and ability to reach them; one who stood high enough to attract the notice of his fellow-men. It seems to me if I were young and in love I should never deem a man of ordinary caliber worthy of my devotion."*

"Now it is you who are telling lies and seeking to deceive me, Mademoiselle; or else you have never been in love, or know nothing about it. Why," went on Edna, clasping her knees and looking up into Mademoiselle's twisted face, "do you suppose a woman knows why she loves? Does she select? Does she say to herself: 'Go to! Here is a distinguished statesman with presidential possibilities; I shall proceed to fall in love with him.' Or, 'I shall set my heart on this musician, whose fame is on every tongue?' Or, 'This financier, who controls the world's money markets?'"

"You are purposely misunderstanding me, ma reine. *Are you in love with Robert?"*

"Yes," said Edna. It was the first time she had admitted it, and a glow overspread her face, blotching it with red spots.

"Why?" asked her companion. "Why do you love him when you ought not to?"

Edna, with a motion or two, dragged herself on her knees before Mademoiselle Reisz, who took the glowing face between her two hands.

"Why? Because his hair is brown and grows away from his temples; because he opens and shuts his eyes, and his nose is a little out of drawing; because he has two lips and a square chin, and a little finger which he can't straighten because he played baseball too energetically in his youth. Because—"

"Because you do, in short," laughed Mademoiselle. "What will you do when he comes back?" she asked.

"Do? Nothing, except feel glad and happy to be alive."

Kate Chopin, *The Awakening*

Neglecting food and sleep

When lovers fall into a state of reverie, such mundane concerns as sleep and nourishment seem to take a low priority. We can see this from the Code of Love in twelfth-century Provence:

> *He whom the thought of love vexes eats and sleeps very little.*
>
> **Andreas Capellanus,** *The Art of Courtly Love*

Indeed, in this state, the besotted lover can become downright lazy while all other pursuits, intellectual and otherwise, seem pale by comparison:

> *This sensation of listlessness, weariness, stupidity, this disinclination to sit down and employ myself, this feeling of everything's being dull and insipid about this house! I must be in love.*
>
> **Jane Austen,** *Emma*

In this fevered stage of infatuation, even constructive work is neglected:

> *Mother dear, I cannot mind my loom*
> *And Aphrodite is to blame:*
> *I'm almost dead*
> *with love-longing for a stripling lad.*
>
> **Sappho,** *The Love Songs*

Stages in the birth of fantasy love:

Fantasy love is not a single state of illusion, but rather an evolution. Our panel of authors, love experts all, will show you the classic steps along the way:

The successive phases of love follow a monotonous course; what they seem to me to resemble most are the endless but sublime repetitions and returns in Beethoven's quartets.

Marguerite Yourcenar, *Coup de Grâce*

Proust believes that fantasy love is actually a succession of little loves:

What we suppose to be our love or our jealousy is never a single, continuous and indivisible passion. It is composed of an infinity of successive loves, of different jealousies, each of which is ephemeral, although by their uninterrupted multiplicity they give us the impression of continuity, the illusion of unity. **Marcel Proust,** *Swann's Way*

Sudden Attraction

Sometimes the initial attraction in fantasy love is the famous infamous *coup de foudre* (bolt of lightning) so well known by characters of flesh and fiction:

Who ever loved, that loved not at first sight? **Christopher Marlowe,** *Hero and Leander*

Or in the haunting words of Sappho:

The moment I saw her
Love
Like a sudden breeze
tumbling on the oak-tree leaves
left my heart
trembling

Sappho, *The Love Songs*

Hope

The next stage of fantasy love is hope, which usually comes in the form of daydreaming about your beloved:

Every act of a lover ends in the thought of the beloved.

Andreas Capellanus, *The Art of Courtly Love*

At first your hopes are modest, a little daydreaming, perhaps. Later on, your thoughts may become more obsessive:

As Edna was walking along the street she was thinking of Robert. She was still under the spell of her infatuation. She had tried to forget him, realizing the inutility of remembering. But the thought of him was like an obsession, ever pressing itself upon her. It was not that she dwelt upon details of their acquaintance, or recalled in any special or peculiar way his personality; it was his being, his existence, which dominated her thought, fading sometimes as if it would melt into the mist of the forgotten, reviving again with an intensity which filled her with an incomprehensible longing. **Kate Chopin,** *The Awakening*

But if all hopes die, so does fantasy love:

Love lives on hope, and dies when hope is dead; it is a flame which sinks for lack of fuel.

Pierre Corneille, *Le Cid*

Doubts about the beloved

But no affair in the mind proceeds without some difficulties. Sooner or later the inevitable doubts filter in to break the euphoria:

*O, how this spring of love resembleth
The uncertain glory of an April day,
What now shows all the beauty of the sun,
And by-and-by a cloud takes all away.*

William Shakespeare, *Two Gentlemen of Verona*

There is nothing people are so often deceived in, as the state of their own affections.

—Jane Austen, Northhanger Abbey

**Zora Neale Hurston
(1891 – 1960)**

The author of **Their Eyes Were Watching God** *was married twice, but both marriages ended in divorce when she refused to give up her traveling and collecting of folk stories to be a stay-at-home wife. Attending Howard University she met Herbert Sheen, also a student, and married him when she was thirty-five. They lived together only eight months. Sheen claimed that the demands of her career doomed the marriage to an early, amicable divorce. In a 1953 letter to Sheen, Hurston recalls the idealistic dreams they shared in their youth, regretting nothing because she lived her life to the fullest.*

A brief second marriage to Albert Price III, in 1939, some fifteen years younger than Hurston, ended less amicably in 1943. Price contended in a divorce countersuit that he feared Hurston's practice of "Black Magic" or "Voodooism."

Undoubtedly there is no pain for the lover like that uncertainty in the early stages:

In the cool of the afternoon the fiend from hell specially sent to lovers arrived at Janie's ear. Doubt. All the fears that circumstance could provide and the heart could feel, attacked her on every side. This was a new sensation for her, but no less excruciating. If only Tea Cake [her man] would make her certain! He did not return that night nor the next and so she plunged into the abyss and descended to the ninth darkness where light has never been.

But the fourth day after he came in the afternoon driving a battered car. Jumped out like a deer and made the gesture of tying it to a post on the store porch. Ready with his grin! She adored him and hated him at the same time. How could he make her suffer so and then come grinning like that with the darling way he had?

Zora Neale Hurston, *Their Eyes Were Watching God*

If you are unsure of your beloved's feelings, you might be tempted to test him, but a test may not be such a great idea. In the following passage from Edith Wharton's *The Reef*, Anna is still unsure of Darrow's love for her:

She felt like testing him by the most fantastic exactions, and at the same moment she longed to humble herself before him, to make herself the shadow and echo of his mood. She wanted to linger with him in a world of fancy and yet walk at his side in the world of fact. She wanted him to feel her power and yet to love her for her ignorance and humility. She felt like a slave, and a goddess, and a girl in her teens.

Edith Wharton, *The Reef*

But beware of such tests. Your beloved may be at a very different stage than you are, and you might be shocked at the results of your test.

Obstacles

For some odd reason, it seems that when your love falls into place *too* easily, it's just not as exciting; a few obstacles may be needed to enhance the value of your love. This curious tendency helps explain the mysterious attraction for those who are different, whether they are from another country or even "the wrong side of the tracks":

...that which typifies the great passion: the immensity of the obstacle to be surmounted and the dark uncertainty of the outcome.

Stendhal, *The Red and the Black*

Sometimes we manufacture difficulties just to make our love more exciting. Even the level headed sometimes long for a few difficulties to enliven their lives. In the following passage from Jane Austen, Elizabeth, the heroine of *Pride and Prejudice*, muses about her love:

"But it is fortunate," thought she, "that I have something to wish for. Were the whole arrangement complete, my disappointment would be certain. But here, carrying with me one ceaseless source of regret in my sister's absence, I may reasonably hope to have all my expectations of pleasure realized. A scheme of which every part promises delight can never be successful; and general disappointment is only warded off by the defense of some little peculiar vexation."

Jane Austen, *Pride and Prejudice*

Indeed, an approving parent or bystander who understands this phenomenon sometimes tries to create some obstacles to make the lovers prove their mettle:

Prospero: They are both in either's pow'rs.
But this swift business
I must uneasy make, lest too light winning
Make the prize light.

William Shakespeare, *The Tempest*

Fortunately there is a bright side. After all these trials and tribulations, if your love comes through, it will actually be worth all the emotional effort you put into it:

> *True is the word that to be cured of fevers*
> *Or other great afflictions men must often*
> *Drink bitter potions, and to have delight*
> *Must swallow many pains and great distress.*
> *But sweetness now seems only the more sweet*
> *For the earlier taste of bitterness; for now*
> *They swim from woe to bliss, and such a bliss*
> *As they had never felt since they were born.*

Geoffrey Chaucer, *Troilus and Cressida*

Anxieties and jealousies

The next stage is that period of "not knowing," the tortuous anxiety of not comprehending the extent of your beloved's interest in you. It is a bittersweet period indeed:

> *In the early stage, love is shaped by desire; later on it is kept alive by anxiety. In painful*
> *anxiety as in desire, love insists on everything. It is born and it thrives only if something*
> *remains to be won.* **Marcel Proust,** *The Captive*

In this anxiety phase, it is best not to over-analyze each word uttered. In the lover's typical fevered state, this can lead only to misinterpretation:

> *Since the utterances of lovers cause them so much anxiety, it would be unwise to jump to*
> *conclusions from any single detail of their conversation. Only in chance remarks are their*
> *feelings reflected; then the heart itself cries out. Apart from this, one can only draw*
> *conclusions from an analysis of the whole pattern of the conversation between the lovers.*
> *It should be remembered that a person under the stress of strong emotions seldom has time*
> *to notice the emotions of whoever is causing them.*

Stendhal, *On Love*

Naturally, your anxiety may lead to jealousy, whether there is ample cause or not:

Jealousy is always born with love, but does not always die with it.
François, duc de La Rochefoucauld, *Maxims*

Unfortunately, jealousy is often the wretched preserve of the person who feels less secure about the relationship, which is a precise definition of one enmeshed in fantasy love. This is an additional burden to add to the anxieties of fantasy love:

He who loves the more is the inferior and must suffer.   **Thomas Mann,** *Tonio Kröger*

Sometimes, jealousy can lead to a mild case of paranoia:

Iago: *Trifles light as air*
Are to the jealous confirmations strong
As proofs of holy writ.   **William Shakespeare,** *Othello*

At worst, such mild paranoia can lead to severe criticism of the beloved:

Jealousy is never satisfied with anything short of an omniscience that would detect the subtlest fault of the heart.... Anger and jealousy can no more bear to lose sight of their objects than love.   **George Eliot,** *The Mill on the Floss*

As we shall see later, it is best to skip over this stage of jealousy—"the green ey'd monster"—as quickly as possible.

Desire for immediate commitment

Finally comes the moment when you (or your lover) cannot contain the silence any longer, and the confession of love bursts forth. Of course, in the first happy moments of confessed love, everything seems possible for the future, especially when you have surmounted the doubts of the past. Note when Troilus and Cressida confess their love for each other:

These two of whom I speak, when in their hearts
They were confirmed in full, they talked and played,
Recalling how and when and where they first
Began to know each other, and each woe
Or fear gone by; but all that heaviness,
I thank God for it, had been turned to joy.
And always when they spoke of a past grief,
That tale was interrupted by a kiss
And turned into fresh joy. Since they were one,
They did their uppermost to be at ease
And counterbalance every outlived woe
By pleasure and recaptured happiness.   **Geoffrey Chaucer,** *Troilus and Cressida*

These tender declarations pour out all the thoughts and anxieties that had bedeviled the lovers in the stage of "not knowing":

When the two lovers perceived that they were of one mind, one heart, and but a single will
between them, this knowledge began to assuage their pain and yet bring it to the surface.
Each looked at the other and spoke with ever greater daring, the man to the maid, the maid
to the man. Their shy reserve was over. He kissed her and she kissed him, lovingly and
tenderly. Here was a blissful beginning for Love's remedy: each poured and quaffed the
sweetness that welled up from their hearts.   **Gottfried von Strassburg,** *Tristan and Isolde*

These trembling confessions naturally lead to expectations of living together happily ever after:

[Adélaide] remained silent and motionless, a prey to a delightful meditation in which all
of her womanly feelings were fused into one. Were they not all summed up in admiration

for the man she loved? When the painter, uneasy at this silence, turned to look at her, she held out her hand to him, unable to say a word. But two tears had fallen from her eyes. Hippolyte took her hand and covered it with kisses. For a moment they looked at each other in silence, both wanting to confess their love and not daring to. The painter kept Adélaide's hand in his. The same warmth and the same agitation told them that their hearts were beating equally strongly. Overcome with emotion, the girl drew gently away from Hippolyte and said, looking at him ingenuously, "You will make my mother very happy."

"What, only your mother?" he asked.

"Oh! I am too happy already."

Honoré de Balzac, *The Purse*

And so all seems to end happily ever after—or at least this is where Harlequin romances or Grade-B Hollywood movies fade into the roseate sunset. But what is the source of all this infatuated madness?

Fantasy love is:

So now we've seen the various systems and stages of fantasy love, as easily identified as any malady in a medical textbook. Where does this happy disorder come from?

A reflection of a desire for connection

Psychologists tell us that infatuation is partially driven by a desire for connection. For example, Ottilie, a young girl in Goethe's novel *Elective Affinities*, falls in love with an older (and married) man largely because her heart desired to connect with someone, anyone, even if the object of her desire was (theoretically) unattainable:

In Eduard she had discovered for the first time what life and joy were, with things as they

**Johann Wolfgang
von Goethe
(1749 – 1832)**

*Reputed to have one
of the highest IQs of all
time, Goethe did not
excel in the ways of
courtship. At the age of
twenty-three, he was
intrigued by the nineteen-
year-old Lotte Buff, who
was engaged to a friend
of his. When Lotte
politely declined his
advances, young Goethe
was heartbroken and
wrote* The Sorrows of
Young Werther *in a mere
four months, a tale of a
rebuffed youth who kills
himself.*

*Later, he became
enamored with Charlotte
von Stein, who was not
only married, but also six
years older and the
mother of three children.
She never became his
mistress despite some
1,500 letters he wrote
to her.*

*Finally, he left Germany
for a trip to Italy, where
he became infatuated
with a lovely young
Milanese lady, only to
find out that she, too, was
engaged! Finally he settled
down with Christine
Vulpius, an attractive and
vivacious younger women
of a lower class. They had
several children before he
married her when he
attained the ripe age of
fifty-seven.*

were now she was conscious of an infinite emptiness of which she hitherto lacked any conception. A heart that is seeking something feels there is something it lacks, a heart that has lost something feels its loss. Desire changes into ill-humor and impatience, and a woman accustomed to wait passively now wants to step out of her usual confines, wants to become active, wants to do something to promote her own happiness.

Johann Wolfgang von Goethe, *Elective Affinities*

A projection of our desires

Not only does love distort the lover's vision of the real character of our beloved, it also can create an illusion of perpetual happiness. In the epistolary novel *Les Liaisons Dangereuses* by Choderlos de Laclos, the wise old Madame de Rosemonde writes to her young confidante Madame de Tourvel:

I thought, my dear, you might find it useful to have these reflections set against those chimerical fancies of perfect happiness with which love never fails to abuse our imaginations; false hopes that one clings to even when one sees that they must perforce be abandoned; the loss of which, moreover, aggravates and multiplies the griefs, all too real already, that are inseparable from deep feeling!

Choderlos de Laclos, *Les Liaisons Dangereuses*

According to Rousseau, the beloved is placed on a pedestal, from which there is only one way to go: down!

And what is true love itself if it is not a chimera, lie, and illusion? We love the image we make for ourselves far more than we love the object to which we apply it. If we saw what we love exactly as it is, there would be no more love on earth. When we stop loving, the person we loved remains the same as before, but we no longer see her in the same way. The magic veil drops, and love disappears.

Jean-Jacques Rousseau, *Emile*

This is why "love" seems to be:

Blind

The most famous symbol of fantasy love is Cupid, that obese diapered cherub whose pathetic little wings manage to keep him aloft through some miracle of levitation. Our chubby friend, armed with a blindfold and a bow, fires arrows of love at hapless and blind lovers. The poor lovers' eyes are then tinctured by the Pollyannish qualities of love, and hence are in no condition to judge reality. Shakespeare is explicit on this theme:

> **Helena:** *Love looks not with the eyes, but with the mind;*
> *And therefore is wing'd Cupid painted blind.*
> *Nor hath Love's mind of any judgement taste;*
> *Wings, and no eyes, figure unheedy haste.*
> *And therefore Love is said to be a child,*
> *Because in choice he is so oft beguil'd.*
>
> **William Shakespeare,** *A Midsummer Night's Dream*

Even rational, well-tempered folks are susceptible to these blinding qualities. We can see this folly—or perhaps generosity of spirit—as Jane Eyre, as level-headed as any woman in literature, falls in love with the master of Thornfield Hall, the gruff Mr. Rochester:

> *I was growing very lenient to my master: I was forgetting all his faults, for which I had once a sharp lookout. It had formerly been my endeavor to study all sides of his character: to take the bad with the good; and from the just weighing of both, to form an equitable judgement. Now I saw no bad. The sarcasm that had repelled, the harshness that had startled me once, were only like keen condiments in a choice dish: their presence was pungent, but their absence would be felt as comparatively insipid.*
>
> **Charlotte Brontë,** *Jane Eyre*

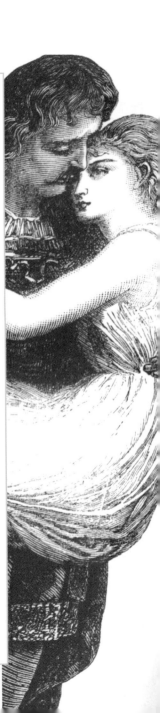

An illusion

   If we are not seeing things as they really are, what *are* we seeing? An illusion, of course. It is an illusion of our own making that elevates our beloved and, in the worst case, distorts our ability to interpret what is really happening:

> *On the moral plane, love is the strongest of the passions. In all the others, desires adopt themselves to cold reality, but in love realities obligingly rearrange themselves to conform with desire.... Hopes and fears at once become* romantic *and* wayward.... *An alarming indication that you are losing your head is that you observe some hardly distinguishable object as white, and interpret this as favorable to your love. A moment later you realize that the object is really black, and you now regard this as a good omen for your love.*
> **Stendahl,** *On Love*

   Since infatuation at this stage is an illusion and we set our beloveds up on a pedestal, we are setting ourselves up for a rude crash to reality when they prove to be mere mortals:

> *To fall in love is to create a religion that has a fallible god.*
> **Jorge Luis Borges,** *The Meeting in a Dream*

   If fantasy love is an illusion, are we lovers merely dupes of nature or victims of an invention of humanity? The cynics would claim that it is nature's fault:

> *I learned that...love was only a dirty trick played on us to achieve the continuation of the species.*
> **W. Somerset Maugham,** *"The Summing Up"*

   But is this illusion all bad? Theodor Reik would argue that it has its beneficial effects:

> *Is love an illusion? Of course it is.... Illusions are also physical realities.... Freud called religion an illusion, but he did not deny that it was an educational factor in the history of mankind.*
> **Theodor Reik,** quoted in the *New York Times*

Folly

But aren't there also countless songs about fools in love? It seems that lovers are not merely blind and deluded, but foolish as well:

Love is apt to make lunatics of even saints and sages.   **Louisa May Alcott,** *Jo's Boys*

Perhaps we place too much faith in rationality. One of the great merits of love is that it can detect virtues in the beloved that others may ignore:

The heart has its reasons which reason does not know.   **Blaise Pascal,** *Pensée 423*

Madness

Plato gave us the wonderful expression "the divine madness" to describe at least one of love's guises, but why "madness"? Are we not still in control of our faculties, although they are altered? Actually, many of our distinguished love experts would argue that fantasy love is a form of temporary insanity:

Rosalind: *Love is merely a madness, and, I tell you, deserves a dark house and a whip as madmen do; and the reason why they are not so punish'd and cured is that the lunacy is so ordinary that the whippers are in love too.*

William Shakespeare, *As You Like It*

John Ford, a contemporary playwright of Shakespeare's, couldn't agree more with the madness thesis, with the same tinge of darkness:

Love is the tyrant of the heart; it darkens
Reason, confounds discretion; deaf to counsel
It runs a headlong course to desperate madness.   **John Ford,** *The Lover's Melancholy*

Now we have read about the symptoms and stages of fantasy love. How about exploring a type of love that has a chance of lasting, like every insipidly romantic song alludes to?

"Romance," Thomas Hart Benton, 1931/32

Mature love: evolution and characteristics

How mature love evolves:

> *Through relaxed friendship*
>
> *Mutual respect*
>
> *Freedom of both parties*
>
> *Natural physical attraction*

Mature love is not easy, but it can offer:

> *Giving and receiving*
>
> *Caring*
>
> *Understanding and forgiving*
>
> *Patience and endurance*
>
> *A journey together*

How mature love evolves:

Let's investigate how we can progress beyond some of the thrills and madness of fantasy love. After all, we should not be slaves to our hearts, merely devoted servants.

Through relaxed friendship

Both Jane Austen and Michel de Montaigne emphasize that relaxed friendship is the cornerstone of any relationship that is going to last. Friendship is also a lot easier than the crazy vicissitudes of fantasy love because you can be who you are and not fake anything:

We who have a mind for the world (whether this be good or bad), how we abuse the days which we squander in Love's name, finding nothing but the self-same crop that we sowed in her—failure and disaster. We do not find the good that each of us desires, and which we are all denied; I mean a steadfast friendship in love, which never fails to comfort us and bears roses as well as thorns and solace as well as trouble. In such friendship joy always lurks among the woes; however often it is clouded, it will bring forth gladness in the end.
Gottfried von Strassburg, *Tristan and Isolde*

Mature love can be modest, without the need to scream its undying devotion:

Authentic love always assumes the mystery of modesty, even in its expression, because actions speak louder than words. Unlike feigned love, it feels no need to set a conflagration.
Honoré de Balzac

Mutual respect

Aretha Franklin was not the only one to recognize that respect is the foundation of any lasting relationship:

The essence of a good marriage is respect for each other's personality combined with that deep intimacy, physical, mental, and spiritual, which makes a serious love between a man and a woman the most fructifying of all human experiences. **Bertrand Russell,** *Marriage and Morals*

Respect should run both ways. Not only do you want your partner to respect you, you should want to respect him. This theme of mutual respect is recurrent throughout Jane Austen's novels, where potential mates become more intriguing to each other as their mutual respect grows. In the following passage from Jane Austen's *Pride and Prejudice*, the heroine's father talked to her about the importance of respect and her upcoming marriage:

I know your disposition, Lizzy. You know that you could never be either happy nor respectable, unless you truly esteemed your husband.... Your lively talents would place you in the greatest danger in an unequal marriage. You could scarcely escape discredit and misery. My child, let me not have the grief of seeing you *unable to respect your partner in life.*
Jane Austen, Pride and Prejudice

Freedom of both parties

For both parties to be able to flourish and grow, they cannot be ordered around like children. Therefore, you should give your partner some freedom and expect it in return:

No human being can ever "own" another, whether in friendship, love, marriage, or parenthood. Many human relationships have been ruined and happiness far too often changed to misery by a failure to understand this.
Eleanor Roosevelt, Book of Common Sense Etiquette

Nor can love grow in an atmosphere of rigid rules and regulations:

Love withers under constraint; its very essence is liberty; it is compatible with neither obedience, jealousy, nor fear: it is there most pure, perfect, and unlimited, where its votaries live in confidence, equality and unreserve. **Percy Bysshe Shelley,** *Queen Mab*

Mature love cannot be coerced, but should have complete freedom of choice:

[Cordelia] must owe me nothing, for she must be free; love exists only in freedom, only in

---

**Jane Austen
(1775 –1817)**

An avid chronicler of English courtship rituals, Austen never married, though she came close several times.

In December 1795, she fell in love with Thomas Langlois Lefroy, a graduate of Trinity College, Dublin, who was visiting his uncle and aunt. Madame Lefroy cut the courtship short by sending her nephew away, recognizing that the young man would be disinherited if he married Jane, the daughter of a penniless clergyman.

About six years later when Jane was twenty-six, she fell in love with a young clergyman while the Austens vacationed on the coast in Devon. The Austens apparently expected that he would propose marriage and be accepted, but he died suddenly.

More than a year later, while visiting her close friends, the Bigg Sisters, their brother proposed to Austen. Because his fortune would ensure her against a fate she feared— spending her old age in poverty—she accepted him even though he was younger and temperamentally unsuited to her. She broke off the engagement the next morning and returned immediately to her parents in Bath.

freedom is there enjoyment and everlasting delight.... She must neither hang on me in the physical sense, nor be an obligation in a moral sense. Between the two of us only the proper play of freedom must prevail. She must be mine so freely that I can take her into my arms.

Søren Kierkegaard, *Either/Or*

Natural physical attraction

Obviously friendship, respect, and freedom are important for mature love, yet it would be ridiculous to insist that these are the sole criteria for a lasting romantic love. After all, how would you distinguish friends from lovers? What is also important is a basic erotic affinity, almost an instinctual desire for the other:

> *It would be mere sophistry to pretend, for instance, that love is or should be nothing but a moral bond, the sympathy of two kindred spirits or the union of two lives. For such an effect no passion would be needed, as none is needed to perceive beauty or to feel pleasure.*

> *What Aristotle calls friendships of utility, pleasure or virtue, all resting on the common interests of some impersonal sort, are far from possessing the quality of love, its thrill, flutter, and absolute sway over happiness and misery. But it may well fall to such influences to awaken or feed the passion where it actually arises. Whatever circumstances pave the way, love itself does not appear until a sexual affinity is declared.*
>
> **George Santayana,** *The Life of Reason*

And the most lasting type of physical attraction is the one that accepts imperfections and loves them all the more:

> *Deeper than the deepest fibre of her vanity was the triumphant sense that as she was, with her flattened hair, her tired pallor, her thin sleeves a little tumbled by the weight of her jacket, he would like her even better, feel her nearer, dearer, more desirable, than in all the splendors she might put on for him. In the light of this discovery she studied her face*

with a new intentness, seeing its defects as she had never seen them, yet seeing them through a kind of radiance, as though love were a luminous medium into which she had been bodily plunged.   **Edith Wharton,** *The Reef*

Mature love is not easy but it can offer:

Perhaps I have painted a halcyon picture of mature love—all roses and no thorns—but as any time-tested lover will tell you, this type of love is never that easy:

For aught that I have ever read,
Could ever hear by tale or history,
The course of true love never did run smooth.   **William Shakespeare,** *A Midsummer's Night Dream*

But mature love offers the consolation that it can be richer and more complex than fantasy love, like an older wine:

All love at first, like a generous wine,
Ferments and frets, until 'tis fine;
But when 'tis settled on the lee,
And from the impurer matter free,
Becomes the richer still, the older,
And proves the pleasanter, the colder.

                                                                   Samuel Butler, *Love*

Giving and receiving

Perhaps the most important thing about mature love (for lovers or parents) is the act of giving, not merely material things, but the self:

Love is an activity, not a passive affect; it is a "standing in," not a "falling for." In the most general way, the active character of love is primarily giving, *not receiving.... Giving*

Therefore love moderately; long love doth so; Too swift arrives as tardy too slow.

—William Shakespeare, Romeo and Juliet

is the highest expression of potency. In the very act of giving, I experience my strength, my wealth, my power. This experience of heightened vitality and potency fills me with joy. I experience myself as overflowing, spending, alive, hence as joyous. Giving is more joyous than receiving, not because it is a deprivation, but in the act of giving lies the expression of my aliveness....

What does one person give another? He gives of himself, of the most precious he has, he gives of his life. This does not necessarily mean that he sacrifices his life for the other—but that he gives him of that which is alive in him; he gives him of his joy, of his interest, of his understanding, of his knowledge, of his humor, of his sadness—of all expressions and manifestations of that which is alive in him. In thus giving of his life, he enriches the other person, he enhances the other's sense of aliveness by enhancing his own sense of aliveness. He does not give in order to receive; giving in itself is the exquisite joy. But in giving he cannot help bringing something to life in the other person, and this which is brought to life reflects back to him; in truly giving, he cannot help receiving that which is given back to him. Giving implies to make the other person a giver also and they both share in the joy of what they have brought to life. In the act of giving something is born, and both persons involved are grateful for the life that is born for both of them. **Erich Fromm,** *The Art of Loving*

And the giving of your *self* is the greatest gift that any lover can receive:

I was gradually, inexplicably, becoming more and more deficient in love, yet better and better at self-giving—the best of loving. **Lawrence Durrell,** *Justine*

Caring

Plato cites tenderness as one of the key ingredients of love and notes that caring releases our tender emotions for the beloved. In Plato's *Symposium*, Agathon explains this softer side of love:

Love is young and also tender; he ought to have a poet like Homer to describe his tenderness; as Homer says of Ate, that she is a goddess and tender:

> *"Her feet are tender, for she sets her steps,*
> *Not on the ground but on the heads of men":*

herein is an excellent proof of her tenderness—that she walks not upon the hard but upon the soft. Let us adduce a similar proof of the tenderness of Love; for he walks not upon the earth, nor yet upon the skulls of men, which are not so very soft, but in the hearts and souls of both gods and men, which are of all things the softest: in them he dwells and makes his home. Not in every soul without exception, for where there is hardness he departs, where there is softness he dwells; and nestling always with his feet and in all manner of ways in the softest of soft places, how can he be other than the softest of soft things?

Plato, *Symposium*

Understanding and forgiving

One of the comforting things about love, whether from family, friends, or lovers, is the feeling of being accepted for who you are, no matter what happens. In the case of romantic love, this acceptance doesn't mean the lover is blind, but rather that he or she accepts the shortcomings and loves anyway:

> *For this is one of the miracles of love; it gives—to both, but perhaps especially to the woman—a power of seeing through its own enchantments and yet not being disenchanted.*

C.S. Lewis, *A Grief Observed*

True love also tends to forgive flaws that otherwise might be difficult to endure. Indeed, sometimes minor flaws in the beloved are loved all the more:

> *Real love accepts people with their weaknesses as well as their strengths. You like to respect and admire someone whom you love, but actually you often love even more the people who*

require understanding and who make mistakes and have to grow with their mistakes.

Eleanor Roosevelt, *My Day*

These acts of forgiveness are the ultimate acceptance of a mate, warts and all, without placing impossible demands on anyone to change:

[Maslow] found in the love of self-actualizing people the tendency to more and more complete spontaneity, the dropping of defenses, growing intimacy, honesty, and self-expression. These people found it possible to be themselves, to feel natural; they could be psychologically (as well as physically) naked and still feel loved and wanted and secure; they could let their faults, weaknesses, physical and psychological shortcomings be freely seen. They did not always have to put their best foot forward, to hide false teeth, gray hairs, signs of age; they did not have to "work" continually at their relationships; there was much less mystery and glamour, much less reserve and concealment and secrecy. In such people, there did not seem to be the hostility between the sexes. In fact, he found that such people "made no really sharp differentiation between the roles and personalities of the two sexes."

Betty Friedan, *The Feminine Mystique*

Ideally, these "tender eyes" of love can also fathom the ideal qualities in the heart and soul of the beloved as well:

True love is rooted in the recognition of the moral and mental qualities of the beloved person.

Richard von Krafft-Ebing, *Pyschopathia Sexualis*

Patience and endurance

Perhaps the most admirable quality of mature love is that it is patient and willing to endure all kinds of trials. In the often-quoted words of St. Paul:

Love is patient and kind; love is not jealous or conceited, or proud; love is not ill-mannered, or selfish, or irritable; love does not keep a record of wrongs: love is not

---

Love is like a baby: it needs to be treated tenderly.

—Proverb from Zaire

Right: "Venus and Adonis," Titian, c. 1560

happy with evil, but is happy with the truth. Love never gives up: its faith, hope and patience never fails. Love is eternal.... There are faith, hope, and love, these three; but the greatest of these is love.   **The New Testament,** *I Corinthians 13*

Unlike the impatience of fantasy love, mature love is durable:

Many waters cannot quench love, neither floods drown it.
                                                         The Old Testament, *Song of Solomon*

Shakespeare speaks poetically of the constancy of true love:

Let me not to the marriage of true minds
Admit impediments. Love is not love
Which alters when it alteration finds
Or bends with the remover to remove.
O, no! it is an ever-fixed mark
That looks on tempests and is never shaken;
It is the star to every wand'ring bark,
Whose worth's unknown, although his height be taken.
Love's not Time's fool, though rosy lips and cheeks
Within his bending sickle's compass come.
Love alters not with his brief hours and weeks,
But bears it out even to the edge of doom.
    If this be error, and upon me prov'd,
    I never writ, nor no man ever lov'd.

                                                         William Shakespeare, *Sonnet CXVI*

A journey together

As has been said many a time by modern philosophers, love is a journey and not a goal. Thus, mature love means growing and progressing together as individuals and as a couple:

The ideal...would be for entirely self-sufficient human beings to form unions one with another only in accordance with the untrammeled dictates of their mutual love.... Love is an ongoing movement, an impulse toward another person, toward an existence separate and distinct from one's own, toward an end in view, a future....

Genuine love ought to be founded on the mutual recognition of two liberties; the lovers would then experience themselves both as self and as other; neither would give up transcendence, neither would be mutilated; together they would manifest values and aims in the world. For the one and the other, love would be revelation of the self by the gift of self and enrichment of the world. **Simone de Beauvoir,** *The Second Sex*

Nor is mature love a journey without potholes and detours. Just as it would be unrealistic to take a cross-country journey without the expectation of some difficulties, any long-term love is bound to experience a few bumps in the road:

Love...is a constant challenge; it is not a resting place, but a moving, growing, working together; even whether there is harmony or conflict, joy or sadness, is secondary to the fact that two people experience themselves from the essence of their existence, that they are one with each other by being one with themselves, rather than fleeing from themselves. There is only one proof for the presence of love: the depth of the relationship, and the aliveness and strength in each person concerned; this is the fruit by which love is recognized. **Erich Fromm,** *The Art of Loving*

So now you know the beginnings of a more mature love. While this type of love lacks some of the excitement and glamour of fantasy love, it does have the chance to perpetuate itself and grow in a healthy fashion. In the next chapter we will explore what men *really* want in both fantasy and mature love.

"La Valse," (The Waltz), Camille Claudel, 1895

What do men want in love? (and not want)

In fantasy love men want:

> *Physical beauty*
>
> *Mystery*
>
> *The chase*
>
> *Madonna and whore*

Why can't men commit?

> *Fear of being trapped*
>
> *Desire for novelty*

In mature love men want:

> *A friend and soulmate*
>
> *Grace and character*
>
> *Kindness*
>
> *An enthusiastic lover*

What do men don't want:

> *Fawning*
>
> *Clinging jealousy*

What do *men want?*

What is it that men, that curious breed, really want? We all know of their insistent carnal desires, but these impulses are often inconstant and capricious. What else do they want?

In fantasy love men want:

For some men, fantasy love is their *only* experience with love. Let's see what this looks like.

Physical beauty

In fantasy love, what often forms the initial attraction for men? Physical beauty, of course. That is what made Romeo moon over Juliet, Petrarch pine for Laura, Dante long for Beatrice. This longing is especially true for young men:

> *Friar Lawrence: Young men's love then lies*
> *Not truly in their hearts, but in their eyes.*   **William Shakespeare,** *Romeo and Juliet*

Even a romantic such as the Irish poet Yeats confesses this manly foible:

> *Wine comes in at the mouth*
> *And love comes in at the eye:*
> *That's all we shall know for truth*
> *Before we grow old and die.*
> *I lift the glass to my mouth,*
> *I look at you, and sigh.*   **William Butler Yeats,** *"A Drinking Song"*

Men seem to be particularly susceptible to physical attractions. Part of the explanation is biological—beauty is most often apparent in women of child-bearing age. Schopenhauer believes that men are most attracted to a particular type of beauty so that they will fall in love and perpetuate the species:

It is a voluptuous illusion which leads the man to believe he will find a greater pleasure in the arms of a woman whose beauty appeals to him than in those of any other; or which indeed, excessively directed to a single individual, firmly convinces him that the possession of her will ensure him excessive happiness. Therefore he imagines he is taking trouble and making sacrifices for his own pleasure, while he does so merely for the maintenance of the species....   **Arthur Schopenhauer,** *The Metaphysics of the Love of the Sexes*

This rather sad, biologically determinist argument has its merits. Yet beyond the "voluptuous illusion," there is an element of aesthetic fascination as well:

Men seemed so hungry for Beauty, hungry for that love which refreshes and inspires without fear or responsibility.   **Isadora Duncan,** *My Life*

Goethe, the great scientist and poet, saw beauty in terms of its beneficial spiritual effects on the beholder:

[Ottilie] became for the men more and more what she had been from the first, which was (to call things by their right names) a feast for the eyes. For if the emerald is through its loveliness a pleasure for the sight, and indeed exerts a certain healing power on that noble sense, human beauty acts with far greater force on both inner and outer senses, so that he who beholds it is exempt from evil and feels in harmony with himself and the world.   **Johann Wolfgang von Goethe,** *Elective Affinities*

Stendhal, as usual, is more philosophic in defining the allure beauty holds for men; he defines it not as an aesthetic or even a lustful attraction as much as a promise of future enjoyment:

But what is beauty? It is a new potentiality for pleasure. Each person's pleasures are different, and often radically so, which explains quite clearly why something that is beautiful to one man is ugly to another.... Let us remember that beauty is the visible expression of character, of the moral make-up of the person; it has nothing to do with passion. Now passion is what we must have, and beauty can only suggest probabilities about a woman and about her self-possession....

Since the beauty a man discovers is a new capacity for arousing his pleasure, and since pleasures vary with the individual, each man's crystallization will be tinged with the colour of his pleasures. The crystallization about your mistress, that is to say her beauty, is nothing but the sum of the fulfillment of all the desires you have been able to formulate about her....

Why does one enjoy and delight in each new beauty discovered in the beloved? It is because each new beauty gives us the complete fulfillment of a desire. We want her to be sensitive: behold! she is sensitive.   **Stendhal,** *On Love*

The paradox of beauty is that it definitely attracts male attention and yet curiously can be intimidating to men:

[Prince Genji] found himself oppressed by the very perfection of her beauty, which seemed only to make all intimacy with her the more impossible.   **Murasaki Shikibu,** *The Tale of the Genji*

Mystery

Undoubtedly, part of the attraction women hold for men is the fact that men often don't understand them. This is partially willful and partially "romantic":

Women, as they are like riddles in being unintelligible, so generally resemble them in this, that they please us no longer once we know them.   **Alexander Pope,** *Thoughts on Various Subjects*

The Swiss psychoanalyst Carl Jung called this mysterious female archetype of attraction the "anima":

> *There are certain types of women who seem to be made by nature to attract anima projections; indeed one could almost speak of a definite "anima type." The so-called "sphinx-like" character is an indispensable part of their equipment, also an equivocalness, an intriguing elusiveness—not an indefinite blur that offers nothing, but an indefiniteness that seems full of promises, like the speaking silence of the Mona Lisa. A woman of this kind is both old and young, mother and daughter, of more than doubtful chastity, childlike, yet endowed with a naive cunning that is extremely disarming to men.*
>
> **Carl Jung,** *The Development of Personality*

For many men in the early stages of fantasy love, mystery is the essence of romance. Once they have "deciphered" a woman, the thrill is gone. Oscar Wilde teases this absurdity in *The Importance of Being Earnest*:

> *Jack: I am in love with Gwendolen. I have come up to town expressly to propose to her.*
> *Algernon: I thought you had come up for pleasure?...I call that business.*
> *Jack: How utterly unromantic you are!*
> *Algernon: I don't see anything romantic about proposing. It is very romantic to be in love. But there is nothing romantic about a definite proposal. Why, one may be accepted. One usually is, I believe. Then the excitement is over. The very essence of romance is the uncertainty. If I ever get married, I shall certainly try to forget the fact.*
> *Jack: I have no doubt about that, my dear Algy. The Divorce Court was especially invented for people whose memories are so curiously constituted.*
>
> **Oscar Wilde,** *The Importance of Being Earnest*

Perhaps the mystery of this absurd attraction is put best by George Bernard Shaw:

> *The fickleness of the women I love is only equaled by the infernal constancy of the women who love me.*   **George Bernard Shaw,** *The Philanderer*

The chase

Foremost, perhaps, men unconsciously and consciously love the chase. Perhaps it is true that all men are unwitting devotees of Artemis, the virgin goddess of the chase. In any event, the chase seems ingrained in the male genetic code. Indeed, even the *Kama Sutra* speaks of this desire as a general law of nature:

> *He does not esteem a woman who is easy to have, but is interested in one difficult to attain.*
> *This is a general rule.*   **Vatsyayana,** *Kama Sutra*

Some poets use the metaphor of the hunt:

> *So the hunter follows the hare, in cold and heat,*
> *On the mountain and along the shore,*
> *But once he has caught it, he cares no more for it,*
> *He only chases what flies from him.*   **Ludivico Ariosto,** *Orlando Furioso*

Nor is this hunting instinct confined to romantic Italians:

> *Man is the hunter; woman is his game.*
> *The sleek and shining creatures of the chase,*
> *We hunt them for the beauty of their skins:*
> *They love us for it, and we ride them down.* **Alfred, Lord Tennyson,** *"The Princess: A Medley"*

Under this strange formulation, the longer the chase, the greater the prize. Indeed, with no chase, there is virtually no value:

> *[True love] is almost entirely lacking when love is inspired by a woman who yields too*
> *soon.... We scorn too easy a victory in love and are never inclined to set much value upon*
> *what is there for the taking.*   **Stendhal,** *On Love*

Indeed, the very skills and strategies necessary for the chase are part of the fascination. Listen to the advice of Mephistopheles to Faust, when the latter sees the lovely and innocent Margaret:

Faust: Had I but seven hours' peace,
I should not need the devil's help
to seduce that darling creature.

Mephistopheles:
You're talking almost like a Frenchman now;
there is no need to be discouraged.
What good is easy consummation?
The pleasure is not half so keen
as when you must first clear your way
through sundry growth and thickets.
Mold your moppet, knead her into shape,
as you have read in those Italian stories.

Faust: Thank you, my appetite is good enough
without such titillations.

Mephistopheles: No nonsense now, I'm serious.
Once for all, the matter is not easy.
You need some time to get this child.
You cannot take the citadel by storm;
we must employ some skill and strategy.

Johann Wolfgang von Goethe, *Faust*

Men who are snared in the stage of fantasy love often revel in the glory of an extended chase:

Think this on the other side: when the sturdy oak
That men have often hacked receives at last
The lucky felling-stroke, with the greater swish
It comes down all at once, as boulders do
Or millstones; for the heavier a thing is,
The swifter is its course when it descends.
The reed that sways and bends with every gust
Lightly enough, the wind gone by, recovers;
But not so an oak when overthrown.

Geoffrey Chaucer, *Troilus and Cressida*

Perversely, perhaps, the more difficult the woman, the more "fun" for the man in love. Jane Austen recognized this peculiar male fancy and had her character Henry explain to his sister, Mary, his fascination for the budding beauty, Fanny:

"I was never so long in company with a girl in my life—trying to entertain her—and succeed so ill! Never met with a girl who looked so grave on me! I must try to get the better of this. Her looks say, 'I will not like you, I am determined not to like you,' and I say she shall."

Jane Austen, *Mansfield Park*

But why is this period of the chase so important? Wouldn't it be easier for all parties if both the man and the woman had a mutual attraction—a simultaneous *coup de foudre*—and came together immediately? Perhaps so, but that would eliminate the period of mystery that is often necessary for the incubation of love. Sometimes an extended chase can even ensnare the hearts of the jaded. This is depicted in *Les Liaisons Dangereuses*, when the Vicomte de Valmont, in writing to his former mistress and partner-in-depravity, the Marquise de Merteuil, unknowingly discloses that he is falling in love with the virtuous Madame de Tourvel:

> *But what is the power that draws me to this woman? Are there not a hundred more who*
> *would be glad of my attentions? Would they not hasten to respond? And though this one*
> *is worth more than they are, has not the attraction of variety, has not the charm of new*
> *conquests, and the glory of their number, pleasures as sweet to offer? Why do we give*
> *chase to what eludes us, and ignore what is at hand? Ah, why indeed?...I don't know, but*
> *I am made to feel it is so.*
>
> **Choderlos de Laclos,** *Les Liaisons Dangereuses*

What is the psychology behind this need to chase? No doubt many a thesis has been written on the topic, but Proust has a simple explanation:

> *We only love what we do not completely possess.*   **Marcel Proust,** *The Captive*

Madonna and whore

Our authors agree that men in the first stages of love enjoy the chase. But what do men want to chase after? The impossible, of course. And what is this impossible yearning?

> *What men desire most is a virgin who is a whore.*   **Edward Dahlberg,** *Reasons of the Heart*

Well, no man has yet found that. What else impossible do they want?

> *We want [women] healthy, vigorous, plump, and chaste— that is to say, hot and cold.*
>
> **Michel de Montaigne,** *Essays*

To borrow from Edith Wharton, just how is "this miracle of fire and ice to be created and to sustain itself in a harsh world?" Simone de Beauvoir points out the unresolvable paradox of men's desire:

> *Just as [the husband] wants [the wife] to be at once warm and cool in bed, he requires her*

*You say,
"I will come."
And
you do not come.
Now you say,
"I will not come."
So I shall
expect you.
Have I learned to
understand you?*

**—Lady Otomo
No Sakanoe**

to be wholly his and yet no burden; he wishes her to establish him in a fixed place on earth and leave him free, to assume a monotonous daily round and not to bore him, to be always on hand and never importunate; he wants to have her all to himself and not to belong to her; to live as one of a couple and to remain alone....

The lover makes the same dual and impossible demands as does the husband: he wants his mistress to be absolutely his and yet a stranger; he wants her to conform exactly to his dream and to be different from anything he can imagine, a response to his expectation and a complete surprise.
                                                  Simone de Beauvoir, *The Second Sex*

Henry James sees a resolution to this paradox: men want their women to be hot with them, but cool with everybody else. In the novella *Daisy Miller* by Henry James, the young American flirt, Daisy—a fascinating blend of audacity and innocence—upsets her lovesick admirer, Winterbourne, with her open behavior with Italian men:

"I am afraid that your habits are those of a flirt," said Winterbourne gravely.
"Of course they are," she cried, giving him her little smiling stare again. "I'm a fearful, frightful flirt! Did you ever hear of a nice girl that was not? But I suppose you will tell me that I am not a nice girl."
"You're a very nice girl; but I wish you would flirt with me, and me only," said Winterbourne.
                                                  Henry James, *Daisy Miller*

D.H. Lawrence has another explanation for these seemingly contradictory desires:

We must remember that man has a double set of desires, the shallow and profound, the personal, superficial, temporary desires, and the inner, impersonal, great desires that are fulfilled in long periods of time. The desires of the moment are easy to recognize, but the others, the deeper ones, are difficult....

But we are very mixed, all of us, and creatures of many diverse and often opposing desires. The very men who encourage women to be most daring and sexless complain most bitterly of the sexlessness of women. The same with women. The women who adore men so tremendously for their social smartness and sexlessness as males, hate them most bitterly for not being "men."

D.H. Lawrence, *A Propos of 'Lady Chatterley's Lover'*

Why can't men commit?

Immanuel Kant, the great German philosopher, argues that men have two puberties: the first puberty allows men to physically create children and the second puberty ensures the moral and intellectual ability to contribute to the care of children. Kant, who reputedly died a virginal bachelor, speculates that at least ten years separate the two puberties. Assuming that Kant's "double puberty" theory is true, why is the time gap between the two puberties so vast? Or more to the point, why can't men commit sooner?

The easy answer is the biological explanation: only 3 percent of all mammals are naturally monogamous. Any reluctant male (or female, for that matter) could legitimately ask: can 97 percent of mammals be wrong? Indeed, Santayana argues that commitment by men is actually counter to their instincts:

Man, on the contrary, is polygamous by instinct, although often kept faithful by habit no less than duty. If his fancy is left free, it is apt to wander.

George Santayana, *The Life of Reason*

On the other hand, the vast majority of human cultures choose monogamy as the basis for marriage. So what's the real reason behind "commitophobia"?

The "Coolidge Effect"

Scientists call the male drive for multiple partners the "Coolidge effect" because of an amusing, though perhaps apocryphal, tale about Calvin Coolidge, U.S. President from 1923 to 1929.

As the story goes, President and Mrs. Coolidge were touring a large farm and separated to inspect different parts of the estate.

At the henhouse, Mrs. Coolidge noticed an amorous rooster chasing a hen and asked the farmer if the rooster mated with the hen every night. When the farmer answered in the affirmative, she requested that he relate this fact to Mr. Coolidge.

When the President reached the henhouse and the farmer dutifully explained the previous conversation, Coolidge calmly asked the farmer if the rooster mated with the same hen every night. When the farmer said no, the President laughed and asked, "Would you please explain that to Mrs. Coolidge?"

Fear of being trapped

The first answer is the fear that they are being "trapped" in terms of their finances and freedom. Arthur Schopenhauer, the lifelong bachelor, (you can see why!), had this to say about marriage:

> *In our monogamous part of the world, to marry means to halve one's rights and double one's duties.... Prudent and cautious men very often hesitate before making so great a sacrifice as is involved in entering into so inequitable a contract.*
>
> **Arthur Schopenhauer,** "On Women"

This fear is not completely without its merits. It would be foolish to enter into financial and/or emotional commitments one cannot fulfill. But I suspect that a more compelling reason men don't commit is something that has little to do with strictly economics, and more with diminished freedom.

Desire for novelty

This second answer is probably the *real* reason why many men can't seem to "pull the trigger," to use that odious expression. The reason resides in this: we men have yet another weakness, an innate interest in "novel females." Scientists call it the "Coolidge effect" and poets call it "inconstancy." Lord Byron asks almost plaintively:

> *...how the devil is it that fresh features*
> *Have such charm for us poor creatures?*
>
> **Lord Byron,** *Don Juan*

Dorothy Parker succinctly states the difference between men and women:

> *General Review of the Sex Situation*

Woman wants monogamy;
Man delights in novelty.

Love is woman's moon and sun;
Man has other forms of fun.
Woman lives but in her lord;
Count to ten, and man is bored.
With this the gist and sum of it,
What earthly good can come of it?

Dorothy Parker, *Enough Rope*

Remember that since the unknown is mysterious, a corollary of this rule can be that a new lover is more exciting than a lover whose qualities are well known. Hence the reluctance to "settle down" with one partner. This is no modern phenomenon either; Thomas of Britain, a writer of the twelfth century, had this to say about the lure of the unknown lover:

A man forsakes the better that is his for the worse that is another's. He considers his own to be inferior, but another's he covets to be better....He expects to find something better than what he has, and so he cannot love his own....But many a man suffers a change of heart and thinks to find in strange things what he cannot find in familiar. So do men's thoughts vary; they wish to try what they lack, and then they have to content themselves. Women do this, too: they abandon what they have for what they fancy and try how they can arrive at their wish and desire. Truly, I do not know what to say on the topic; but men and women equally are too much enamored of novelty, for they change too often their inclinations, their desires, and their wishes against reason and possibility.

Thomas of Britain, *Tristran and Ysolt*

In mature love men want:

Surely not all men are incapable of commitment. Thousands of men around the world get married every day, for a variety of reasons. Now that we have seen the folly of distortions created by fantasy love, let us take a look at what makes men want in a more mature relationship.

**Edith Wharton
(1862 –1937)**

Edith Wharton, the great chronicler of social convention and hypocrisy, suffered from that milieu herself. In April 1885, at twenty-five, she began a disastrous marriage to Edward Wharton—a union in which she keenly felt the social imprisonment of being part of high society. The two were divorced after twenty-eight years of marriage in 1913. Perhaps the most passionate experience of Wharton's life was a brief but intense affair with Morton Fullerton, a ne'er-do-well American journalist living in Paris.

A friend and soulmate

Eventually, after men realize that the impossible does not exist, they begin to search for a mate, someone with whom they can start a family. In *Jane Eyre*, Mr. Rochester describes his ten-year search for a wife:

> *My fixed desire was to seek and find a good and intelligent woman, whom I could love....
> You are not to suppose that I desire perfection, either of mind or person. I longed only for
> what suited me....*   **Charlotte Brontë,** *Jane Eyre*

Ideally, this "search" comes through a process of getting to know someone over an extended period of time:

> *It was during their night walks back to the farm that [Ethan] felt most intensely the
> sweetness of this communion. He had always been more sensitive than the people about
> him to the appeal of natural beauty. His unfinished studies had given form to this
> sensibility and even in his unhappiest moments field and sky spoke to him with a deep and
> powerful persuasion. But hitherto the emotion had remained in him a silent ache, veiling
> with sadness the beauty that evoked it. He did not even know whether any one else in the
> world felt the way he did, or whether he was the sole victim of this mournful privilege.
> Then he learned that one other spirit trembled with the same touch of wonder: that at his
> side, living under the same roof and eating his bread, was a creature to whom he could
> say: "That's Orion down yonder; the big fellow on the right is Aldebaran, and the bunch
> of little ones—like bees swarming—they're the Pleiades...."*

> *[A]nd there were other sensations, less definable but more exquisite, which drew them
> together with a shock of silent joy: the cold red of sunset behind winter hills, the flight of
> cloud-flocks over slopes of golden stubble, or the intensely blue shadows of hemlocks on
> sunlit snow. When [Mattie] said to him once: "It looks just as if it was painted!" it seemed
> to Ethan that the art of definition could go no further, and that words had at last been
> found to utter his secret soul....*   **Edith Wharton,** *Ethan Frome*

With such a "soulmate" a man can share his hopes and fears:

[T]he real fierceness of desire, the real heat of a passion long continued and withering up
the soul of a man is the craving for identity with the woman that he loves. He desires to
see with the same eyes, to touch with the same sense of touch, to hear with the same ears,
to lose his identity, to be enveloped, to be supported. For, whatever may be said of the
relation of the sexes, there is no man who loves a woman that does not desire to come to
her for the renewal of his courage, for the cutting asunder of his difficulties. And that will
be the mainspring of his desire for her. We are all so afraid, we are all so alone, we all
so need from the outside the assurance of our own worthiness to exist.

Ford Madox Ford, *The Good Soldier*

In the end, this type of soul bonding is the true "beauty":

The union of the souls is a thousand times more beautiful than that of bodies.

Abu Muhammad ibn-Hazm, *The Ring of the Dove*

Grace and character

Many great writers, such as Rousseau, recognized the primacy of character over more
ephemeral attractions:

Graces do not wear out like beauty. They have life, they are constantly renewed, and at the
end of thirty years of marriage, a decent woman with grace pleases her husband as she did
on the first day.   **Jean-Jacques Rousseau,** *Emile*

Even a rake like Ovid understood the importance of grace and character:

Your first concern, girls, should be for proper behavior:
With a fine personality, features are sure to please.
Love of character's lasting, but age will ravage beauty,
The pretty face wrinkle and line,

Till a time will come when you'll hate to look in the mirror,
And misery etches those furrows deeper still.
But probity lasts well, will endure for ages, can carry
Love with its weight of years.   **Ovid,** *"On Facial Treatment for Ladies"*

Kindness

While sharing of dreams is important, the act of giving and receiving kindness every day is vital for a healthy relationship:

It's not beauty but
Fine qualities, my girl, that keep a husband.   **Euripides,** *Andromache*

Or, as expressed by an idealistic lad, who is clearly not ensnared in fantasy love:

Petruchio: *Kindness in women, not their beauteous looks,*
Shall win my love.   **William Shakespeare,** *The Taming of the Shrew*

Indeed, kindness is the basis for any relationship:

There is nothing that cannot be accomplished
without affection and kindness, or rather love.   **Cicero,** *Epistulae ad Familiares*

An enthusiastic lover

Men, of course, want a lover in their mate, but an enthusiastic lover is especially delightful:

There's no satisfaction for a man, unless the woman shares it.   **Aristophanes,** *Lysistrata*

D.H. Lawrence, an avid proponent of sexual freedom, argues that a significant part of a man's satisfaction comes from pleasing his woman in bed. In Lawrence's novel *Lady*

Chatterley's Lover, Oliver Mellors, the gamekeeper, confesses his need for a satisfied lover to his mistress, Lady Constance Chatterley:

"And you talk so coldly about sex," she said. "You talk as if you had only wanted your
own pleasure and satisfaction."
She was protesting nervously against him.
"Nay!" he said. "I wanted to have my pleasure and satisfaction of a woman, and I never
got it: because I could never get my pleasure and satisfaction of her unless she got hers of
me at the same time. And it never happened. It takes two."

D.H. Lawrence, *Lady Chatterley's Lover*

Ovid, who fancied himself a connoisseur on the subject, is characteristically more verbose:

I can't stand a woman who puts out because she has to,
Who lies there dry as a bone
With her mind on her knitting. Pleasure by way of duty
Holds no charms for me, I don't want
Any dutiful martyrs.
I love the sighs that betray their rapture,
That begs me to go slow, to keep it up
Just a little longer. It's great when my mistress comes, eyes swooning,
Then collapses, can't take any more....

Ovid, *The Art of Love*

What men don't want:

Now we've reviewed what men want in mature love. What is that they *don't* want?

Fawning

According to the literature (and my own experience), the first characteristic men don't want is a woman who is too eager, too obsequious. This behavior might be pleasant for a very short period, but after a while it is exasperating. Partially this is because with the passage of time, cloying behavior becomes nauseating. Perhaps more important for those crucial first impressions, a fawning woman doesn't need to be chased. In *Pride and Prejudice*, we can see an illustration of the value of speaking one's own mind when Elizabeth is talking to Darcy, her fiancé:

> *"Now be sincere; did you admire me for my impertinence?"*
> *"For the liveliness of your mind, I did."*
> *"You may well call it impertinence at once. It was very little less. The fact is you were*
> *sick of civility, of deference, of officious attention. You were disgusted with the women*
> *who were always speaking and looking and thinking for* your *approbation alone. I roused,*
> *and interested you, because I was so unlike* them. *Had you not been so amiable you would*
> *have hated me for it; but in spite of your pains you took to disguise yourself, your feelings*
> *were always noble and just; and in your heart, you thoroughly despised the persons who*
> *so assiduously courted you."*
>
> **Jane Austen,** *Pride and Prejudice*

Later in a relationship, groveling can be absolutely fatal to love. In *Madame Bovary*, Emma's increasingly obsequious attachment to her lover, Rodolphe, ends up revolting him:

> *She was becoming terribly sentimental. They had to exchange miniatures and cut off locks*
> *of their hair, and she was now asking him for a ring, a real wedding ring, as a symbol of*
> *their eternal union....*
>
> *While [Rodolphe's] bourgeois common sense was disdainful of her exalted raptures, in his*
> *heart he found them delightful, since it was he who inspired them. Eventually, sure of her*
> *love, he stopped making any special effort to please her, and little by little his manner*
> *changed.*

He no longer spoke to her in words so sweet they made her weep, and there were no more of the fiery caresses that threw her into a great frenzy. Their great love, in which she lived totally immersed, seemed to be subsiding around her, like the water of a river sinking into its bed, and she could see the mud of the bottom. Refusing to believe it, she redoubled her tenderness; and Rodolphe hid his indifference less and less.

She did not know whether she regretted having given in to him or whether, instead, she wished she could love him more. Her humiliating awareness of her own weakness was turning into resentment, which was tempered by her voluptuous pleasures. It was not an attachment, it was kind of continuous seduction. She was under his domination. She was almost afraid of him.   **Gustave Flaubert,** *Madame Bovary*

One of the great killers of love occurs when our lovers turn servile; in a way servility degrades love itself, for how can we continue to love someone who grovels? In Virgil's *The Aeneid*, Dido, the proud Queen of Carthage, begs Aeneas not to leave her, to no avail:

She now felt driven to weep again, again
To move him, if she could, by supplication,
Humbling her pride before her love—to leave
Nothing untried, not to die needlessly.   **Virgil,** *The Aeneid*

How pathetic! Surely this is the point at which pride should reassert itself, if only to prevent the depressing picture that Simone de Beauvoir paints of the woman who loses herself in love:

Giving herself blindly, woman has lost the dimension of freedom which at first made her fascinating. The lover seeks his reflection in her; but if he begins to find it altogether too faithful, he begins to get bored. It is again one of the loving woman's misfortunes that her very love disfigures her, destroys her; she is nothing more than this slave, this servant, this too ready mirror, this too faithful echo. When she becomes aware of this, her distress reduces her worth still further; in tears, demands, and scenes she succeeds in losing all her attractiveness....

[Man] preaches to woman that she should give—and her gifts bore him to distraction; she is left in embarrassment with her useless offerings, her empty life. On the day when it is possible for woman to love not in her weakness but in her strength, not to escape herself but to find herself, not to abase herself but to assert herself—on that day love will become for her, as for man, a source of life and not of mortal danger.

Simone de Beauvoir, *The Second Sex*

Clinging jealousy

The other great aversion for men is women who cling too closely; it is too constricting. After the initial euphoria of always being together wears off, men seem to need some room to breathe. Once again there is a fine line to tread; a *little* jealousy is acceptable—indeed, who can trust a lover who is *never* jealous?

[Anna] was glad now that she had confessed all her doubts and her jealousy. She divined that a man in love may be flattered by such betrayals, that there are moments when respect for his liberty appeals to him less than the inability to respect it: moments so propitious that a woman's very mistakes and indiscretions may help to establish her dominion.

Edith Wharton, *The Reef*

But the line can be crossed if an occasional jealous outburst threatens to become possessive. In D.H. Lawrence's *Women in Love*, Birkin (who mirrors much of Lawrence's thinking) reflects on the possessiveness of the two women in his life, Hermione and Ursula:

But it seemed to him, woman was always so horrible and clutching, she had such a lust of possession, a greed of self-importance in love. She wanted to have, to own, to control, to

"Quadrille at the Moulin Rouge," Henri de Toulouse-Lautrec, 1892

be dominant. Everything must be referred back to her, to Woman, the Great Mother of everything, out of whom everything must be finally rendered up....

D.H. Lawrence, *Women in Love*

No doubt Lawrence exaggerates, but the material point here is that men can get claustrophobic when women seem to be too grasping. Simone de Beauvoir is a little less apocalyptic but conveys the essential point:

[The woman in love] gives herself to [her lover] entirely; but he must be completely available to receive this gift. She dedicates every minute to him, but he must be present at all times; she wants only to live in him—but she wants to live, and he must therefore devote himself to making her live.... At first the woman in love takes delight in gratifying her lover's desire to the full; later on—like the legendary fireman who for love of his profession started fires everywhere—she applies herself to awakening this desire so that she may have it to gratify...it comes in the form of a gift, when it is really a tyranny....

Simone de Beauvoir, *The Second Sex*

What may seem to de Beauvoir to be a woman's passionate tyranny simply may be the need to be reassured of love, although for the man such insistent questioning can be tiresome. In a considerably less somber vein, Oscar Wilde with his usual satirical wit reveals in a conversation between three young dandies how a woman's cool behavior is attractive, but utter devotion is tedious:

Dumby: She really doesn't love you, then?

Lord Darlington: No, she does not!

Dumby: I congratulate you, my dear fellow. In this world there are only two tragedies. One is not getting what one wants, the other is getting it. The last one is the worst, the last is the real tragedy! But I am interested to hear that she does not really love you. How long could you love a woman who didn't love you, Cecil?

Cecil Graham: *A woman who didn't love me? Oh, all my life!*

Dumby: *So could I. But it's so difficult to meet one.*

Lord Darlington: *How can you be so conceited, Dumby?*

Dumby: *I didn't say it as a matter of conceit. I said it as a matter of regret. I have been wildly, madly adored. I am sorry I have. It has been an immense nuisance. I should like to be allowed a little time to myself now and then.*

Oscar Wilde, *Lady Windermere's Fan*

You have now seen a little of what men want and don't want in both mature and fantasy love. The next step is how to put this knowledge into action, as we shall examine in the next chapter.

D ating advice for women: Avoiding the pitfalls of fantasy love

Initial strategies for starting a relationship:

> *Be natural, not bubbly*
>
> *Chat, don't chase*
>
> *Affect a little coolness...but don't be too cool*
>
> *Don't give in too quickly*
>
> *Don't let him get too confident*
>
> *Let him pay...just don't borrow or lend*

Initial strategies for starting a relationship:

Now you are armed with the knowledge of the complicated desires of men, particularly when they are ensnared by the contradictory desires of fantasy love. What can you do about it, particularly in the initial sensitive stages of getting to know somebody? Indeed, the first stages are fraught with many pitfalls:

There is hardly any activity, any enterprise, which is started with such tremendous hopes and expectations, and yet fails so regularly, as love.   **Erich Fromm,** *The Art of Love*

Left: "Love's Young Dream," Jennie Augusta Brownscombe, 1887

If the tentative first steps to achieving love fail so often, and the stakes are so high, what should you do about it? Cervantes urges a little strategizing to aid the process of courting:

We have no right to exact vengeance for the wrongs love does to us. Remember that love and war are the same thing, and since it is permissible in war to make use of stratagems to overcome the enemy, so in the contests of love the tricks and wiles employed to achieve the end desired are allowable, provided they do not bring injury or dishonor on the beloved one.   **Miguel de Cervantes,** *Don Quixote*

Thus, strategizing is fair game. Let's examine what our panel of love experts advises.

Be natural, not bubbl

By all means, establish contact! There's absolutely nothing wrong with initiating eye contact or flirting first. In fact, anthropologists tell us that in the vast majority of cultures (including our own), women are generally the first to establish eye contact and then look away. Let's say you see a man who excites your interest. Your first impulse may be to approach him merely to talk. This is fine—just restrain yourself from being too bubbly or enthusiastic. Not only does that become tiresome, it seems naïve:

Girls bubbling over with the most innocent gaiety become the most tedious of women in less than a year.   **Stendhal,** *On Love*

Of course, a little enthusiasm is always a welcome addition to any social situation, but in moderate doses, please! Ovid believes that too much sweetness can be a bit sickening:

Sweetness cloys the palate
Bitter juice is a freshener.   **Ovid,** *The Art of Love*

Frankly, even a little shyness is preferable to relentless cheerfulness:

You want to make him interested in you? Then act embarrassed in his presence....
                                    Friedrich Nietzsche, *Beyond Good and Evil*

And don't try to be something you aren't. In the end, the best advice is to be yourself:

For she had come to feel that it was the only thing worth saying—what one felt.
Cleverness was silly. One must simply say what one felt.   **Virginia Woolf,** *Mrs. Dalloway*

It doesn't make sense to change your opinions or personality to suit the situation, because you are not presenting yourself as you really are. Dorothy Parker puts it best, as usual, quite bluntly:

In youth, it was a way I had
  To do my best to please,
And change, with each passing lad,
  To suit his theories.

But now I know the things I know,
  And do the things I do;
And if you do not like me so,
  To hell, my love, with you!

                                            Dorothy Parker, *"Indian Summer"*

Being natural includes going easy on the makeup:

I clearly saw Edna withdrawing hurriedly from the front room as I drove up. Women!
No matter how beautiful they are they always try to be more—and usually fail; though in
Edna's case she was great with face powder and the rest, and great without them.
                                            Chinua Achebe, *A Man of the People*

**Virginia Woolf
(1882 – 1941)**

One of the great practitioners of stream-of-consciousness, Woolf was sexually abused at a young age by both her half-brothers, a trauma sometimes blamed for her later descent into madness. She had numerous affairs with women (most notably Vita Sackville-West) before marrying Leonard Woolf, a fellow member of the celebrated Bloomsbury Group. Her affairs with Sackville-West escalated during her marriage, while Leonard took male lovers. Nevertheless, the marriage was reputed to be a happy one, though they had no children and Virginia suffered from periodic bouts of depression. She attempted suicide several times, finally succeeding in drowning herself, like Ophelia in Hamlet, in 1941.

You should avoid obviously seductive outfits as well; it looks cheap as well as desperate:

She wore far too much rouge last night and not enough clothes. That is always
a sign of despair in a woman.   **Oscar Wilde,** *An Ideal Husband*

Modesty is particularly important as one gets older:

Gaga was perhaps showing a bit too much, particularly in view of the fact that at her age
she would have done better not to have shown anything at all.   **Emile Zola,** *Nana*

Chat, don't chase

After the initial, natural conversations, your next impulse may be to plan out all sorts of future endeavors together. By all means, keep planning. Just don't unburden all these dreams on your shy swain all at once. Learn to take your time:

Few people bare their feelings at the outset of any relation; we generally try to show off our
exterior, as a tree its bark, to the best advantage.   **Honoré de Balzac**

Recall the basic premise that men seem to need the chase. Much as men may like to be approached, they feel awkward when they are openly pursued. Ovid concisely explains this familiar paradoxical mentality of men:

I flee who chases me, and chase who flees me.   **Ovid,** *The Amores*

This advice may sound frustrating to women who want to take the first initiative—but there is a residual nugget of enduring truth: men do not take seriously what comes too easily. So what can an ardent, pro-active woman do? One tactic is to follow the footsteps of Molly, the pert young seducer of Tom Jones:

[Molly] liked Tom as well as he liked her, so when she perceived his backwardness she

*grew proportionately forward; and when she saw that he had entirely deserted the house,
she found means of throwing herself in his way and behaved in such a way that the youth
must have been very much or very little of the hero if her endeavours had proved
unsuccessful. In a word, she soon triumphed over all the virtuous resolutions of Jones; for
though she behaved at last with all decent reluctance, yet I rather choose to attribute the
triumph to her, since, in fact, it was her design which succeeded. In the conduct of this
matter Molly so well played her part that Jones attributed the conquest entirely to himself,
and considered the young woman as one who yielded to the violent attacks of his passion.*

Henry Fielding, *Tom Jones*

However, this balancing act between active pursuit and coyness is very tricky, because
you can't make your efforts seem too obvious or reveal your passion too soon, as we shall
see shortly.

Affect a little coolness...

Overt chasing is out. So what else do our writers suggest? Interestingly enough,
sometimes a little dose of coolness can pique a man's curiosity or his sense of vanity. After
all, playing coy is a time honored mating technique practiced by females of many species.
Speaking strictly of human mating techniques, writers as diverse as Ovid, Jane Austen, and
Susan Sontag all note that men are actually encouraged by the occasional polite rebuff.
Marcel Proust suggests using the deliberate tactic of putting off your suitor:

*Indeed, among the lesser auxiliaries to success in love, an absence, the declining of an
invitation to dinner, an unintentional, unconscious harshness are of more service than all
the cosmetics and fine clothes in the world.*   **Marcel Proust,** *The Guermantes Way*

At first glance, this strategy seems strange, because normally we are put off by people
who are rude to us. But budding love is an entirely different world, and all the rules are
upside down. Lady Murasaki explains the curious convolutions of the male heart thusly:

It is in general the unexplored that attracts us, and [Prince] Genji tended to fall most

---

*Our heart is a
treasury; if you
spend all its
wealth at once
you are ruined.*

**—Honoré
de Balzac,
*Le Pere Goriot***

*in love with those who gave him the least encouragement. The ideal condition for
the continuance of his affection was that his beloved, much occupied elsewhere, should
grant him no more than the occasional favour.*   **Murasaki Shikibu,** *The Tale of the Genji*

Why should this paradox exist? Shouldn't the heart be attracted to that which desires it?
Apparently the heart is not at all a rational organ. Perhaps it is because men love a mystery
and they can't comprehend why any woman wouldn't love them! One way to get around
this paradox is to make the budding lover work for a favorable smile in his direction:

*A lover should pave the way with letters: make sure you detail
    A trustworthy maid to act as your go-between.
Examine each message, deduce from his own expressions
    Whether it's faked, or written with genuine
Heartfelt distress. Wait a little before you reply: a lover's
    Honed up by delay—provided it's not too long.
Don't yield too easily to a lover's entreaties,
    But, equally, don't overdo
Those stubborn refusals. Scare him, yet leave him hopeful;
    Let each letter reduce his fear, increase his hopes.*   **Ovid,** *The Art of Love*

Therefore, alternate doses of aloofness and encouragement seem to be best. But at all
costs, don't reveal your interest too early; this would defy the dictum of being cool. Or as
Lucetta, the wise old maid to Julia in *Two Gentlemen of Verona*, advises:

*Fire that's closest kept burns most of all...
O, they love least that let men know their love.*

William Shakespeare, *Two Gentlemen of Verona*

From an earlier source, the Code of Love from the twelfth century in Provence, we find:

Who knows not how to conceal knows not how to love.

Andreas Capellanus, *The Art of Courtly Love*

And from a slightly more modern (and sardonic) source:

Lady, lady, never speak
Of the tears that burn your cheek
She will never win him, whose
Words had shown she feared to lose.   **Dorothy Parker,** *"The Lady's Reward"*

Whatever you do, don't tip your hand too early! It ruins the mysterious period of incubation for the man, the sweet pain of not knowing how his beloved feels.

...but don't be too cool

In his role as one of the world's first biologists, Aristotle was often wrong, but never in doubt. For example, he fearlessly states that a man's sperm is active, while a woman's egg is passive. Modern science, on the other hand, demonstrates that a woman's egg has to coax the directionless and blind sperm through the release of an attracting enzyme. Using nature as an analogy, a woman should not feel inhibited from using her natural charms to attract a reluctant mate.

But given what we know of the natural reticence of men in the face of overt chasing, it is best not to seem overly eager. On the other hand, you can't be too disdainful, either. Jane Austen suggests that being too reserved may give the wrong impression. In Austen's *Pride and Prejudice*, Charlotte advises:

It is sometimes a disadvantage to be so very guarded. If a woman conceals her affection
with the same skill from the object of it, she may lose the opportunity of fixing him; and it
will then be poor consolation to believe the rest of the world equally in the dark. There is

> **There is safety in reserve, but no attraction. One cannot love a reserved person.**
>
> **—Jane Austen, *Emma***

Ovid
(43 B.C. – 17 A.D.)

The author who was called praeceptor amoris ("instructor on love") by the Romans, was first married at eighteen, quite common for a young man of his time, but the marriage ended in divorce in less than two years. His first wife was probably fourteen when she married. He later characterized his first wife rather ungenerously as "neither worthy nor useful."

After numerous affairs, he was pressured by his father to marry again, and this time he fathered a daughter before his wife died, probably in childbirth. In contrast with his treatment of his first wife, he went out of his way to praise the second wife in his writings.

At age forty-three, around the time of the publication of The Art of Love, *he married a third time, this time to a previously married woman in her thirties. She was politically well connected, but her connections did not prevent Ovid from being exiled from Rome on charges of lewd writings, notably* The Art of Love *and* The Amores. *His wife stayed behind in Rome to win a reprieve from his banishment, but she failed and Ovid died alone in Tomis, a Roman outpost on the Black Sea.*

so much of gratitude or vanity in almost every attachment that it is not safe to leave any to itself. We can all *begin freely—a slight preference is natural enough; but there are very few of us who have enough to be really in love without encouragement. In nine cases out of ten, a woman had better show* more *affection than she feels.*

Jane Austen, *Pride and Prejudice*

Dorothy Parker laments that by a woman's not saying anything to her would-be beau, there is not much of a chance of any kind of relationship beginning:

So silent I when Love was by
   He yawned, and turned away;
But Sorrow clings to my apron-strings,
   I have so much to say.

Dorothy Parker, *"Anecdote"*

Ovid, as usual, is more than ready to offer advice on how to tread this fine line between frostiness and fawning:

It does just as much harm to look haughty—
A gentle expression will best
Encourage love. I detest—and believe me, I know it—
the over
Disdainful air: too often a silent face
Holds the seeds of hatred. Return his smiles and glances;
If he beckons, acknowledge the gesture with a nod...
What else? Glum girls are a bore. Leave Ajax to Tecmessa:
We men are a cheerful breed, it's bright
Girls who charm us best.

Ovid, *The Art of Love*

But it doesn't make much sense to be too proud, anyway, because as time goes by, it is but a small consolation to be able to say, "He was once crazy about me":

Do not forget how age wastes hour by hour
Some portion of your beauty; love, then, do,
Before you are consumed by age. Once old,
No one will heed you. Be ruled by the proverb:
"Aware too late," said of beauty as it withered.
Age tames disdain at last. The king's fool shouts
Whenever a woman puts on airs: "Live long,
You in your pride, until crow's feet come
Under your eyes; and then go find a glass
To see yourself in the morning."

Geoffrey Chaucer, *Troilus and Cressida*

And don't make the mistake of spurning a man just because he is available—that fact alone doesn't mean that something must be wrong with him. In the following passage from Chinua Achebe, a young woman contemplates the desirability of Chris, a young man she met:

I recall clearly that the very first time we met the thought that flashed through my mind was
to be envious of his wife. And yet it was weeks before I could bring myself to probe
delicately about her, not directly through Chris but surreptitiously via a third party, Ikem.
But such was the carefully balanced contrariness induced in me by Chris that the news of
his wife's nonexistence, though it admittedly gave me a measure of relief, did not bring total
satisfaction. There was a small residue of disappointment at the bottom of the cool draught,
so they say. Was it the disappointment of the gambler or the born fighter cheated out of the
intoxication of contest and chancy victory? Or did the affair lose some of its attraction for
me because deep inside I was not unlike the dreadful, cynical aunt in the village who
believed that nothing so good could wait this long for me to stumble upon? What an awful
thought!

Chinua Achebe, *Anthills of the Savannah*

Perhaps the biggest shame of all is that undue pride can deprive you of what we all need:

When heaven has endowed you with a soul made for love, not to love is to deprive yourself and others of great happiness. It is as if an orange-tree dared not to flower for fear of committing a sin. And remember that a soul made for love can never be satisfied with any other kind of happiness.   **Stendhal,** *On Love*

Don't give in too quickly

Suppose there's an attractive man who gives you a nice smile while passing in the hallway. In a matter of seconds, you might contemplate whether he is available and whether he will ask you out. Or perhaps even a little more?

A lady's imagination is very rapid; it jumps from admiration to love, from love to matrimony, in a moment.   **Jane Austen,** *Pride and Prejudice*

Even if your imaginary musings do come true and he asks you out, don't be too obvious about wanting to move forward. Consistent with the desire of men for the chase and some sense of mystery, it seems obvious that the longer the chase lasts, the greater the charm:

The easy attainment of love makes it of little value; difficulty of attainment makes it prized.   **Andreas Capellanus,** *The Art of Courtly Love*

Therefore, in the interest of long-term romance, you have to show some restraint:

The duration of a couple's passion is in proportion to the woman's original resistance or the obstacles that social hazards have placed in the way of her happiness.

Honoré de Balzac

Even the *Kama Sutra*, well known for its erotic advice, echoes this theme:

When you are propositioned, you must never accept at once. Men have no esteem for easy women.   **Vatsyayana,** *Kama Sutra*

Thus it is imperative to the germination of love not to give in too soon:

Leave off hungry. One ought to remove the bowl of nectar from the lips. Demand is the measurement of value.... The only way to please is to revive the appetite by the hunger that is left. If you must excite desire, better to do it by the impatience of want than by the surfeit of enjoyment. Happiness earned gives double joy.

Balthasar Gracián, *The Art of Worldly Wisdom*

But why is this so? The wily Wife of Bath believes it is because men always prize what is most expensive and most difficult to attain. In the "Prologue to the Wife of Bath's Tale," she explains to her fellow pilgrims:

We're chary of what we hope men will buy.
A throng at market makes the prices high;
Men set no value on cheap merchandise,
A truth all women know if they are wise.

Geoffrey Chaucer, *The Canterbury Tales*

Stendhal has a more sophisticated explanation. He believes that the heart essentially needs an incubation period for love to properly develop. For this reason, in his book, *On Love*, he preaches the virtues of (some) modesty on the part of women:

Modesty protects love by imagination, and so gives it a chance to survive.... As for the purpose of modesty, it is the mother of love; that is enough to justify it.... Modesty both pleases and flatters a lover, for it lays stress on the laws which are being transgressed for his sake.

Stendhal, *On Love*

Stendhal, *nom de plume* of
Marie-Henri Beyle
(1783 – 1842)

The romantic author of
On Love *and* The Red and
the Black *was not very lucky
in love. Born to a bourgeois
family in Grenoble, France,
he distinguished himself for
bravery in Napoleon's army.
Later he traveled around
France and Italy as a
functionary and journalist,
finally obtaining a post as a
French consul in one of the
chief ports of the Papal
States near Rome. He was
fat, not particularly
handsome, and a hopeless
romantic.*
  *After multiple failed
affairs, he spent his middle
age pining after Mathilde
Viscounti Dembowski, a
lovely Italian countess
separated from her Polish
husband. She only allowed
Stendhal to visit her every
few weeks, thereby inflaming
his infatuation. He wrote* On
Love *partially as an effort to
dissect his own passion, as
well as to attract Mathilde's
admiration. Apparently she
was not impressed—the
affair remained one-sided
and was never consummated.
Despite his lifelong
preoccupation with passionate love, Stendhal died a
bachelor at the age of
fifty-nine.*

All of these arguments for modesty seem quaint yet fairly convincing; in any event, the tired old bromide of "Don't give in too soon" uttered by every parent is not without some validity.

Don't let him get too confident

I may be betraying the short-term pleasure characteristic of my gender, but the simple truth is that if we men get too sure of a woman's affections in the initial stages of dating we tend to lose interest. Don't ask me why, but complacency seems to be the greatest enemy in sustaining love. The heart is a strange creature; and a love that is *too* sure seems to lose that keen edge of desire necessary to sustain the flame. To be sure, trust is the cornerstone of any sustaining love, but a *little* doubt seems to be the piquant sauce that enlivens the budding relationship. Thus the advice—given by a wide range of male writers, from the cynics to the romantics—suggests that you should always leave him a little room for doubt. Call it the "2 percent rule": 98 percent confidence and 2 percent doubt. Or as Stendhal paraphrases the musings of one of his female correspondents:

> *Always a little doubt to set at rest, that's what keeps the craving, that's what keeps happy love alive. Because the misgivings are always there, the pleasures never grow tedious.*
> **Stendhal,** *On Love*

Ovid, on the other hand, would seem to prefer the "50 percent rule"; 50 percent hope and 50 percent doubt:

> *We lovers need hope and despair in*
> *Alternate doses. An intermittent rebuff*
> *Makes us promise the earth....*

> *Act thus, and my love will endure, grow stronger with each passing*
> *Year—that's the way I like it, that feeds the flame,*
> *Love too indulged, too compliant, will turn your stomach*

Like a surfeit of sweet rich food.

To prolong your dominion over
Your lover calls for deception. (I hope I won't
Have cause to regret that statement.) Yet come what may,
indulgence
Irks me. I flee the eager, pursue the coy.   **Ovid,** *The Amores*

Personally, I don't condone outright deception, like Ovid suggests, but a little mystery or faint suspicion of other admirers (again, only in those crucial early stages) is admittedly intriguing. Ovid expands on his theory and suggests that even if you don't actually have active admirers, you can always invent some competition:

Don't let him get cocksure, without any rivals:
Love minus competition never wears well.
Leave the bed suspiciously rumpled, make sure he sees it,
Flaunt a few sexy bruises on your neck—
Above all, show him his rival's presents (if none
are forthcoming
Order some yourself, from a good shop).   **Ovid,** *The Amores*

These delicious moments of doubt can be agonizing, as well as intoxicating for men:

If Fabrizio had not loved her so well he would have clearly seen that he was loved; but he
had very grave doubts about this matter.... Fabrizio's life was fully occupied. It was entirely
taken up with seeking the solution to this important problem: "Does she love me?" The
result of innumerable observations, perpetually renewed, but as perpetually subject to
misgivings, was as follows: "All her deliberate gestures say 'No,' but every involuntary
movement of her eyes seems to admit that she is becoming fond of me."
                                   Stendhal, *The Charterhouse of Parma*

Any man, however blasé or depraved, finds his love kindled anew when he sees himself threatened by a rival.

—Honoré de Balzac

Not that I'm suggesting extended mystery or deception, but just don't let the early dating phase slide into a regular routine:

Love, like fire, cannot survive without continual movement; it ceases to live as it ceases to hope or fear.   **François, duc de La Rochefoucauld,** *Maxim 75*

Let him pay...just don't borrow or lend

Numerous studies have shown that a primary source of friction in marriage is money. Money can also be a defining element in the courting process, so you have to be careful during that period as well:

True lovers know how trifling a thing is money yet how difficult to blend with love!
                                                                        Honoré de Balzac

During the early dating stage, if a man asks you out, he should pay. After all, he did the inviting! On the other hand, never—repeat, never—borrow or lend money. This almost inevitably poisons the process of true love from developing:

Between lovers the sharing of money increases love; the giving of money destroys love.
In one case present misfortune and, for the future, the grim prospect of the fear of want are dismissed; in the other case an element of politics is introduced, an awareness of being two which negates fellow-feeling.   **Stendhal,** *On Love*

"Neither a borrower nor a lender be" is doubly true for lovers; monetary disputes are a sure recipe for amorous disaster. As Flaubert notes:

Of all the winds that blow on love, none is more chilling and destructive as a request for money.   **Gustave Flaubert,** *Madame Bovary*

Whatever you do, don't demand gifts from your lover. He may consent, but the joy of giving vanishes for the giver. No doubt tired of being asked for gifts from his mistress, Ovid adds this exasperated complaint:

> *Do mares demand gifts from their stallions? Do cows solicit*
> *Their bulls? Must a ram*
> *Court ewes with their offerings? Only a woman a glories*
> *In fleecing her males. She alone*
> *Rents out her nights, is up for bids, plays the seller's market,*
> *Lets her pleasure adjust the price.*
> *When sex gives equal pleasure to both partners*
> *Why should she sell it, he pay?*
> *If a man and a woman perform the same act together, is it*
> *Fair for you to profit by it, while I lose....*
> *From each*
> *Lover his all—but according to his resources....*
> *I'm not ungenerous, it's being*
> *Asked I detest. Quit wanting, and I'll give.*
>
> **Ovid,** *The Amores*

The moral is, if at all possible, keep money questions out of the picture. Love is difficult enough without introducing financial considerations!

So let's assume that you've avoided all the pitfalls of fantasy love during the dating stage. In the next chapter we shall find out if this is the right man for you.

Pair Statue of Mycerinus and Queen Kha-merer-Nebty II, Egypt, 2548-2530 B.C.

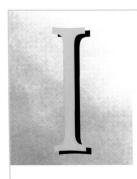

Is this the right man for you?

How to pick the right man:

    Make sure he is available!

    Get to know your partner well

    A friend and companion

    Shared goals and interests

    Complementary characters

    Compatible sense of humor

    Sexual chemistry

How not to pick a mate:

    Out of desperation

    Don't be blinded by money or status

    Solely on the basis of physical attraction

    As a "good match"

When you still can't decide...

    Get away for a while

How to pick the right man:

Let's face it, the odds confronting a modern couple contemplating marriage are daunting: half of all marriages end in divorce, and many others are virtually inert, on auto-pilot but devoid of a mature and growing love. The choice of whom you marry is one of the most important decisions you can make in life. It determines with whom you are going to live, share good times and bad, and raise children. On the other hand, you can't expect perfection in your mate. You want to stay single? Keep searching for the perfect mate!

In many cultures, the decision for a spouse is made by one's parents. In fact, it is a relatively recent development in the annals of human affairs to assume that a love attraction between a young couple has anything to do with the choice of a spouse. Traditionally, a spouse was chosen to maximize the social and economic standing of the offspring—a rational, and decidedly unromantic, proposition. Nowadays, of course, we tend to seek "love matches," though this seems to lead to divorces more often than "arranged" marriages.

Does it make any sense to weigh all the options before marriage? After all, if we choose to look at the statistics or all the potential pitfalls, a "rational" decision would be to forestall any move until we were "sure":

Once we ask ourselves what is involved in choosing a man or a woman for the rest of one's life, *we see that to choose is to wager. Both in the lower and middle classes the wiseacres urge young men "to think it over" before taking the decisive step. They thus foster the delusion that the choice of wife or husband may be governed by a certain number of accurately weighable pros and cons. This is a crude delusion on the part of common sense. You may try as you like to put all the probabilities at the outset in your own favour—and I am assuming that life allows you the spare time for such nice calculations—but you will never be able to foresee how you are going to develop, still less how the wife or husband you choose is going to, and still less again how the two of you together are going to.*   **Denis de Rougemont,** *Love in the Western World*

Of course, some mating choices are not so well planned. Consider the "bride-races" of many older Asian and European cultures:

> [T]here is one race, called the "Love Chase," which may be considered a part of the form of marriage among the Kirghiz. In this the bride, armed with a formidable whip, mounts a fleet horse, and is pursued by all the young men who make pretensions to her hand. She will be given as a prize to the one who catches her, but she has the right, besides urging her horse on to the utmost, to use her whip, often with no mean force, to keep off those lovers who are unwelcome to her, and she will probably favour the one she has already chosen in her heart....
>
> Similar customs appear to have been practiced by all Teutonic peoples; for the German, Anglo-Saxon, and Norse languages possess in common a word for marriage which simply means bride-race. Moreover, traces of the custom survived into modern times.
>
> **Sir James George Frazer,** *The Golden Bough*

However intriguing this method of choosing a mate, I would suggest that you pursue a slightly more conventional approach. Of course, Carl Jung would argue that our so-called rational selection is but an illusion:

> As a rule the motives [a lover] acts from are largely unconscious. Subjectively, of course, he thinks himself very conscious and knowing, for we constantly overestimate the existing content of consciousness.... The greater the area of unconsciousness, the less is marriage a matter of free choice, as is shown subjectively in the fatal compulsion one feels so acutely when one is in love.
>
> Unconscious motivations are of a personal and of a general nature. First of all, there are the motives deriving from parental influence. The relationship of the young man to his mother, and of the girl to her father, is the determining factor in this respect. It is the strength of the bond to the parents that unconsciously influences the choice of husband or

*A great flame
follows
a little spark.*

**—Dante Alighieri,
The Divine
Comedy**

wife, either positively or negatively. Conscious love for either parent favours the choice of a like mate, while the unconscious tie (which need not by any means express itself consciously as love) makes the choice and imposes characteristic modifications....

Generally speaking, all the life which the parents could have lived, but of which they thwarted themselves for artificial motives, is passed on to the children in substitute form. That is to say, the children are driven in a direction that is intended to compensate for everything that was left unfilled in the lives of their parents. Hence it is that excessively moral-minded parents have what are called "unmoral" children, or an irresponsible wastrel of a father has a son with a positively morbid amount of ambition, and so on.

Carl Jung, *The Development of Personality*

Unconscious motivations notwithstanding, it would be foolish not to look for a few key characteristics in a potential spouse, and perhaps more important, to avoid certain temptations when deciding on a partner. On a more jocular note, Benjamin Franklin suggests:

Keep your eyes wide open before marriage, half shut afterwards.

Benjamin Franklin, *Poor Richard's Almanack*

Ultimately, it seems to me (based on my observations) that the biggest single mistake one can make is to choose a mate based on our desires rather than our needs. So what are the basic needs?

Make sure he is available!

This should be obvious, but an all too common prelude to heartbreak is getting involved with an unavailable man. No matter how attracted you are to a man, if he is married or dating someone else, you are setting yourself up for a very painful situation. Just remind yourself that it is impossible for a healthy and mature love to flourish in a love triangle. If one (or both) partners are splitting their time and emotional energy with others, by definition they cannot concentrate on making a relationship work with you:

A love affair can prosper only when both parties enter free. If one lover is free and the other not, then in the process of destroying their rival or memory of their rival, the one who is free will destroy the illusion of their own virtue....

Axiom: There is no happiness to be obtained by the destruction of another's. To take wife away from husband or husband away from wife is a kind of murder; guilt turns lovers into bad accomplices and the wrecking of a home destroys the wreckers. As we leave others, so shall we be left.   **Cyril Connelly,** *The Unquiet Grave*

Get to know your partner well

Since it is such an important decision, it is well worth taking the time to really get to know the person with whom you want to spend your future. This means not just in the (usually) halcyon setting of the dating world, but also in spending lots of informal time together. From Chaucer's "The Merchant's Tale" we get the following advice about choosing a spouse:

It's no child's play
To take a wife without investigation.
It ought to be your earnest occupation
To find out whether she is wise or lazy,
Sober or drunk or shrewish or man-crazy,
Rich or poor or wasteful; and though it is a folly
To look for anything unblemished wholly
In this world, man or beast, a wife who had
A few more virtuous qualities than bad
Ought to suffice. But that takes time to learn.   **Geoffrey Chaucer,** *The Canterbury Tales*

Plato, who never married, argues that it is critical to learn about the other's family:

[W]hen people are going to live together as partners in marriage, it is vital that the fullest possible information should be available about the bride and her background and the

Geoffrey Chaucer
(1342 – 1400)

After a long bachelorhood of service to the crown, the writer of the famous Canterbury Tales *married well to Philippa Roet, a knight's daughter who received a lifetime annuity for her service to the queen. If one can read into the advice given about marriage in* Canterbury Tales, *the marriage was not overwhelmed with domestic felicity. Nevertheless, the union did produce two children before Philippa's sudden death.*

family she'll marry into. One should regard the prevention of mistakes here as a matter of supreme importance....
                                                                    Plato, *The Laws*

Another significant question to ask yourself is: do you like your partner's friends? Do they like you? This answer is important because friends are a realistic reflection of the type of person your partner really is.

A friend and companion

Since you are going to share so much time together with your mate, with all the inevitable problems and aggravations that life provides, it makes sense that friendship form the core of the relationship:

The best friend is likely to acquire the best wife, because a good marriage is based on the talent for friendship.... When marrying, one should ask oneself this question: Do you believe you will be able to converse with this woman into your old age?
                                            Friedrich Nietzsche, *Human, All Too Human*

Another way of looking at the question of durability is to ask yourself "Do I want this man to be the father of my children?" and "Would I want my son to grow up to be like this man?" This is a very different way of looking at your mate than just asking "Has this guy been a good boyfriend?"

Shared goals and interests

One often overlooked aspect of the marriage decision is the importance of having basically congruent goals. This is especially important in the key issue of whether or not to raise a family, and, if so, how both partners plan to contribute to the all-important task of rearing children. If both partners are not in agreement on these basic issues, they could end up pulling in different directions:

As concerning marriage, it is certain that this is in harmony with reason, if the desire for physical union be not engendered solely by bodily beauty, but also by the desire to beget children and to train them up wisely; and moreover, if the love of both, to wit, of the man and the woman, is not caused by bodily beauty only, but also by freedom of soul.

Baruch Spinoza, *Ethics*

Complementary characters

Although it may or may not be true that opposites attract, certainly possessing complementary characters can be more harmonious in the long run. One way of thinking about character is to look for a spouse who complements you, not competes with you:

[I]t is definitely better for the virtue of a man and wife if they balance and complement each other than if they both are at the same extreme. If a man knows he's rather headstrong and apt to be too quick off the mark in everything he does, he ought to be anxious to ally himself to a family of quiet habits, and if he has the opposite kind of temperament he should marry into the opposite kind of marriage.   **Plato,** *The Laws*

Aristotle and Plutarch—both of whom had happy marriages—also stress the importance of friendship and complementary personalities for a successful marriage. When these characteristics are present, no one spouse is overwhelming:

When a match has equal partners
Then I fear not.   **Aeschylus,** *Prometheus Bound*

More philosophically, this type of arrangement is probably the best for both partners to progress:

The moral regeneration of mankind will only really commence when the most fundamental of the social relations [marriage] *is placed under the rule of equal justice, and when human beings learn to cultivate their strongest sympathy with an equal in rights and in cultivation.*

John Stuart Mill, *"The Subjugation of Women"*

Compatible sense of humor

Often overlooked in the search for a lifelong partner is a marriage of minds and humor, which is indispensable for any enduring friendship:

> *The real marriage of true minds is for any two people to possess a sense of humor or irony pitched in exactly the same key, so that their joint glances at any subject cross like interarching searchlights.*   **Edith Wharton**, *A Backward Glance*

In fact, different types of humor can actually cause tension between partners:

> *A difference in the taste of jokes is a great strain on the affections.*
> **George Eliot,** *Daniel Deronda*

Sexual chemistry

Although respect, trust, and friendship are important, these can be found, with luck and work, outside of marriage. What makes a particular relationship special is the addition of some thing extra, like sexual chemistry within the framework of loving:

> *Automatons cannot love; they can exchange their "personality packages" and hope for a fair bargain. One of the most significant expressions of love, and especially of marriage with this alienated structure, is the idea of "team." In any number of articles on happy marriage, the ideal described is that of a smoothly functioning team. This description is not too different from the idea of a smoothly functioning employee; he should be "reasonably independent," co-operative, tolerant, and at the same time ambitious and aggressive.... All this kind of relationship amounts to is the well-oiled relationship between two persons who remain strangers all their lives, who never arrive at a "central relationship," but who treat each other with courtesy and who attempt to make each other feel better.*

> *In this concept of love and marriage the main emphasis is on finding refuge from an*

otherwise unbearable sense of aloneness. In "love" one has found, at last, a haven from aloneness. One forms an alliance of two against the world, and this egotism à deux is mistaken for love and intimacy. **Erich Fromm,** *The Art of Loving*

In fact, too much concern about the personality can undermine the very important basis for sexual chemistry:

Modern people are just personalities, and modern marriage takes place when two people are "thrilled" by each other's personality: when they have the same tastes in furniture or books or sport or amusement, when they love "talking" to one another, when they admire one another's "minds." Now this, this affinity of mind and personality is an excellent basis for friendship between the sexes, but a disastrous basis for a marriage. Because marriage inevitably starts the sex activity, and the sex activity is, and always was and will be, in some way hostile to the mental, personal relationship between man and woman. It is almost an axiom the marriage of two personalities will end in startling physical hatred. People who are personally devoted to one another at first end by hating one another with a hate which they cannot account for, which they try to hide, for it makes them ashamed, and which is none the less only too painfully obvious, especially to one another. In people of strong individual feeling the irritation that accumulates in marriage increases only too often to a point of rage that is close akin to madness. And, apparently, all without reason. But the real reason is that the exclusive sympathy of nerves and mind and personal interest is, alas, hostile to blood-sympathy in the sexes. The modern cult of personality is excellent for friendship between the sexes, and fatal for marriage.

D.H. Lawrence, *A Propos of 'Lady Chatterley's Lover'*

How not to pick a mate:

If there are certain positive facets to look for in a man, it follows that there are other traits or reasons to get married that you should avoid.

Out of desperation

While it is certainly true that the biological clock is less forgiving for women than for men, this is no reason to panic and get married to any man who presents himself. In particular, you should do your best to resist the social pressure to marry just to be married. In Chinua Achebe's *Anthills of the Savannah*, Beatrice, a young, attractive and intelligent woman in Nigeria, speaks of the pressure to get married:

Chris was not a Commissioner when I met him but a mere editor of the National Gazette. *That was way back in civilian days. And if I say that Chris did all of the chasing I am not boasting or anything. That was simply how it was. And I wasn't being coy either. It was a matter of experience having taught me in my lonely world that I had to be wary. Some people even say I am suspicious by nature. Perhaps I am. Being a girl of maybe somewhat above average looks, a good education, a good job, you learn quickly enough that you can't open up to every sweet tongue that comes singing at your doorstep. Nothing very original really. Every girl knows that from her mother's breast although thereafter some may choose to be dazzled into forgetfulness for one reason or another. Or else they panic and get stampeded by the thought that time is passing them by. That's when you hear all kinds of nonsense talk from girls: Better to marry a rascal than grow a moustache in your father's compound; better an unhappy marriage than an unhappy spinsterhood; better to marry Mr. Wrong in this world than wait for Mr. Right in heaven; all marriage is* how-for-do; *all men are the same; and a whole bag of foolishnesses like that.*

Chinua Achebe, *Anthills of the Savannah*

Don't panic and marry just anyone for the sake of marriage and "security":

[Varenka] must have been fed up with such a life and longed for a home of her own. Besides, there was her age; there was no time left to pick and choose; she was apt to marry anybody, even a teacher of Greek. Come to think of it, most of our young ladies don't care whom they marry so long as they do marry.

Anton Chekhov, *"The Man in a Shell"*

On the other hand, you shouldn't marry someone just to shock or spite others either. After all, you're the one who has to live with your husband, not your parents:

Her marriage to Léonce Pontellier was purely an accident, in this respect resembling many other marriages which masquerade as the decrees of Fate. It was in the midst of her secret great passion that she met him. He fell in love, as men are in the habit of doing, and pressed his suit with an earnestness and an ardor which left nothing to be desired. He pleased her; his absolute devotion flattered her. She fancied there was a sympathy of thought and taste between them, in which fancy she was mistaken. Add to this the violent opposition of her father and her sister Margaret to her marriage with a Catholic, and we need seek no further for the motives which led her to accept Monsieur Pontellier for her husband.... She grew fond of her husband, realizing with some unaccountable satisfaction that no trace of passion or excessive and fictitious warmth colored her affection, thereby threatening its dissolution.
                                                           Kate Chopin, *The Awakening*

Don't be blinded by money or status

One particular trap for women is to choose a mate based on his social status rather than the strength of his character or other important attributes:

[Florence] wanted to marry a gentleman of leisure; she wanted a European establishment. She wanted her husband to have an English accent, an income of fifty thousand dollars a year from real estate and no ambitions to increase that income.... [She] was coldly and calmly determined to take no look at any man who could not give her a European settlement. Her glimpse of English home life had effected this. She meant, on her marriage, to have a year in Paris, and then have her husband buy some real estate in the neighbourhood of Fordingbridge.... On the strength of that she was going to take her place in the ranks of English country society. That was fixed.
                                                  Ford Madox Ford, *The Good Soldier*

Although this choice is myopic, at least it is one woman's own volition. In much sadder circumstances, many women throughout history have been pressured by poverty to pursue rich men in order to survive. Consider the wretched situation of Lily, the lovely protagonist of Edith Wharton's *The House of Mirth*:

> *[Lilly] had been bored all afternoon by Percy Gryce—the mere thought of him seemed to waken an echo of his droning voice—but she could not ignore him on the morrow, she must follow up her success, must submit to more boredom, must be ready with fresh compliances and adaptabilities, and all on the bare chance that he might ultimately do her the honour of boring her for life....*
>
> *She returned wearily to the thought of Percy Gryce, as a wayfarer picks up a heavy load and toils on after a brief rest. She was almost sure that she had "landed" him: a few days' work and she would win her reward. But the reward itself seemed unpalatable just then: she could get no zest from the thought of victory. It would be a rest from worry, no more— and how little that would have seemed to her a few years earlier! Her ambitions had shrunk gradually in the desiccating air of failure. But why had she failed? Was it her fault or that of destiny?*
>
> *She remembered how her mother, after they had lost all their money, used to say to her with a kind of fierce vindictiveness: "But you'll get it all back—you'll get it all back, with your face...."*
> **Edith Wharton,** *The House of Mirth*

On the other hand, you shouldn't be unnaturally prejudiced *against* those with wherewithal; just don't make it the foundation of the relationship:

> *He'd have given me rolling lands,*
> *Houses of marble, and billowing farms,*
> *Pearls, to trickle between my hands,*
> *Smoldering rubies, to circle my arms,*
> *You—you'd only a lilting song,*

Only a melody, happy and high,
You were sudden and swift and strong—
Never a thought for another had I.

He'd have given me laces rare,
Dresses that glimmered with frosty sheen,
Shining ribbons to wrap my hair,
Horses to draw me, as fine as a queen.
You—you'd only whistle low,
Gayly I followed wherever you led.
I took you, and let him go—
Somebody ought to examine my head!

Dorothy Parker, *"The Choice"*

Solely on the basis of physical attraction

A common trap of many relationships is to assume because a passionate physical attraction exists now, it will last forever. Jane Austen throws cold water on this passionate notion:

How little of permanent happiness could belong to a couple who were only brought together because their passions were stronger than their virtue.   **Jane Austen,** *Pride and Prejudice*

George Bernard Shaw even ridicules the notion that lust can last:

When two people are under the influence of the most violent, most insane, most delusive and most transient of passions, they are required to swear that they will remain in that exalted, abnormal, and exhausting condition until death do them part.

George Bernard Shaw, *Getting Married*

Even Montaigne, hardly a prude, warns young lovers about the longer-term perils of physical attraction as the sole means of choosing a mate:

He may say that he loves you. Wait and see what he does for you!

—Proverb from Senegal

**Michel de Montaigne
(1533 – 1592)**

The "father of the essay" married Françoise de la Chassaigne when he was thirty-two. They had six children, though tragically only one survived more than a few months. Montaigne famously argued that friendship, not love, should be the foundation for marriage. His own marriage was widely believed to be a solid family match and without pretensions to passion. As he grew older, he became quite attached to Marie de Gournay, a young woman who became executor and editor to his literary estate. Although his relationship with Marie was unclear, he wrote that he loved her "more than a daughter," which she later edited to "as a daughter."

I see no marriage fail sooner or have more troubles than such as are concluded for beauty's sake, and huddled up for amorous desire....   **Michel de Montaigne,** *Essays*

As a "good match"

Perhaps the most common mistake in making a marriage decision comes from choosing to marry the type of person we *want* to marry rather than the type we *need*. By this I mean that we formulate a package of wants in a partner and opt for the best "package" that we can find in exchange for our own "package." Thus we see that many of the youngest marriages are between high school jocks and cheerleaders, the highest rungs on the ladder of perceived male and female success. According to the social theories of Konrad Lorenz, the primary social success attributes are money and success for men and beauty and youth for women. Accordingly, it is no surprise to see these combinations together strolling through any airport or luxury resort. (Obviously the trend does not all go one way— sometimes we see "trophy husbands" as well, though not nearly as often.)

The problem with this matching is that while the packages may be socially equal, there is not necessarily equality within the marriage. Erich Fromm states this frame of mind in terms of exchange in an elaborate meat market:

Our whole culture is based on the appetite for buying, on the idea of a mutually favorable exchange. Modern man's happiness consists in the thrill of looking at the shop windows, and in buying all that he can afford to buy, either for cash or on installments. He (or she) looks at people in a similar way. For the man an attractive girl—and for the woman an attractive man—are the prizes they are after. "Attractive" usually means a nice package of qualities which are popular and sought after on the personality market. What specifically makes a person attractive depends on the fashion of the time, physically as well as mentally....

At any rate, the sense of falling in love develops usually only with regard to such human commodities as are within reach of one's own possibilities for exchange. I am out for a bargain; the object should be desirable from the standpoint of its social value, and at the same time should want me, considering my overt hidden assets and potentialities. Two persons thus fall in love when they feel they have found the best object available on the market, considering the limitations of their own exchange values.

Erich Fromm, *The Art of Loving*

At best this type of union leads to boredom:

[W]ith a shiver of foreboding, [Archer] saw his marriage becoming what most other marriages around him were: a dull association of material and social interests held together by ignorance on the one side and hypocrisy on the other.

Edith Wharton, *The Age of Innocence*

At worst such an "exchange" is doomed to failure; because each party is seeking to maximize its own happiness, the union as a whole necessarily suffers:

The friendship of utility is full of complaints; for as they use each other for their own interests they want to get the better of the bargain, and they think they have got less than they should, and blame their partners because they do not get all they "want and deserve"....

[I]n the friendship of lovers sometimes the lover complains that his excess of love is not met by love in return (though perhaps there is nothing lovable about him), while often the beloved complains that the lover who formerly promised everything now performs nothing. Such incidents happen when the lover loves the beloved for the sake of pleasure while the beloved loves the lover for the sake of utility, and they do not possess the qualities expected of them. If these be the objects of the friendship it is dissolved when they do not get the things that formed the motives of their love; for each did not love the other person himself but the qualities he had, and these were not enduring; and that is why the friendships are also transient.

Aristotle, *Nichomachean Ethics*

When you still can't decide...

If you still can't decide about the man after weighing all the pros and cons, perhaps you should listen to your internal doubts:

If a woman doubts as to whether she should accept a man or not, she certainly ought to refuse him. If she can hesitate as to "Yes," she ought to say "No" directly. It is not a state to be entered into with doubtful feelings, with half a heart.   **Jane Austen,** *Emma*

Your indecision could be a signal that you are not ready to settle down with this particular man:

[I] think a woman who is undecided between two offers, has not love enough for either to make a choice; and in that very hesitation, indecision, she has a reason to pause and seriously reflect, lest her marriage, instead of being an affinity of souls or a union of hearts, should only be a mere matter of bargain and sale, or an affair of convenience and selfish interest.   **Frances E. W. Harper,** *"The Two Offers"*

Get away for a while

If you're still not sure, getting away for a short period might help you decide if this relationship was meant to last:

Absence diminishes mediocre passions and increases great ones, as the wind blows out candles and fans fire.
                                        François, duc de La Rochefoucauld, *Maxim 276*

And after your travels and ruminations, if it turns out that this one is not the right man for you, be patient. Something will happen, but not when you expect it:

They made such a romantic voyage across the Mediterranean and through the sands of Egypt to the harbour of Bombay, to find only a gridiron of bungalows at the end of it. But she did not take the disappointment as seriously as Miss Quested, for the reason that she was forty years older, and had learnt that Life never gives us what we want at the moment that we consider it appropriate. Adventures do occur, but not punctually.

E.M. Forster, *A Passage to India*

You have thus seen how to choose the right man, or, just as important, how to avoid the wrong man for you. Now let's explore one of the most delightful aspects of a healthy relationship: making love.

Frances E. W. Harper (1825 – 1911)

One of the most prolific and well known African-American authors of the nineteenth-century, Frances Ellen Watkins Harper was also active in the abolitionist movement just prior to the Civil War. In the midst of these often dangerous activities, she published The Two Offers, *which argued that marriage is an option, not a neccessity, for a woman.*

A year later, at age thirty-five, she married Fenton Harper, a widower with three children, and moved to a farm in Ohio. Unfortunately, her husband died not long after their daughter Mary was born. Harper then took to the lecture circuit to support her family, where she spoke alongside such luminaries as Soujourner Truth, Susan B. Anthony, and Frederick Douglass.

"Lovers (Mithuna)," India, Madyha Pradesh, Khajuraho style, 11th century

Making love

Don't confuse love and lust

Respect your partner

Be spontaneous

Be generous

Let yourself go

Show your pleasure

Take your time

Praise your partner

Making love

No doubt many readers jumped straight to this chapter before reading the preceding chapters. (Perhaps you, Passionate Reader?) But there's no need to rush; by speeding up the process, you are missing the best part of making love: the thrill of sharing intimacies with the one you love. That's why this chapter is called "Making Love" and not "Unleash Your Lust!," to quote a memorable headline from a woman's magazine.

Of course the lusty act is known by a great number of euphemisms: "an ecstatic unity" (Simone de Beauvoir), "loving swallows" (Li T'ung Hsüan), "the bottom-kicking dance" (Aristophanes), "climbing the tree" (Vatsyayana), "the sports of love" (Ben Jonson), and "liquid desire" (Homer). But these crude approximations allude only to the corporal instincts (fun as they are) and not to the greater delights of sharing and making love.

Curiously, making love has quite different qualities in traditional Western and Eastern philosophies. For most Western societies, sex and spirituality are quite separate concepts, and are often considered mutually exclusive. In contrast, many Eastern cultures embrace sexuality as a part of their spiritual practice, as well as a joyful method to promote general health and well-being.

Don't confuse love and lust

The first big mistake is that we tend to confuse our hormonal instincts for mating with the loftier sentiments of love. Sex can be simply a release of tension and have little to do with bringing a couple closer. (In fact, the word "sex" comes from "sexus," the Latin word meaning "split.") Noting the tension between passion and friendship, Montaigne gives a pithy definition of lust:

> *[The flame of passion] is more active, hotter, and fiercer [than friendship.] But it is a*
> *reckless and fickle flame, wavering and changeable, a feverish fire prone to flare up and*
> *die down, which only catches us in one corner.*   **Michel de Montaigne,** *Essays*

Stendhal, a true philosopher of love, mentions one more unfortunate trait about that seemingly unloved beast: lust. It is the crude fact that lust is quite temporary, and not much on which to base a long-term relationship:

> *The more physical pleasure plays a basic part in love and in what initially brought about*
> *the intimacy, the more liable that love is to inconstancy and, still more, to unfaithfulness.*
>   **Stendhal,** *On Love*

It is not merely that lust is ultimately futile; it is also that experiencing true love is incomparably better:

I learned a little too late that, as the Duc d'Albe said, one salmon is worth more than a thousand frogs! To be sure, a genuine love affair gives a thousand times more happiness than the ephemeral passions one arouses.   **Honoré de Balzac,** *"Domestic Peace"*

Katherine Anne Porter, in a letter to her nephew who had recently mustered out of the army, preferred to think that sex and love belonged in two distinct camps, with neither holding a particular advantage:

You mentioned that, in the midst of your recent drunken revelries, such a change from the chaste rule of the armed forces, you have "rediscovered Sex—the Foul Kind." Dear me, what other kind is there? You must tell me more at once. Of course, times do change and vocabularies change, too, but in my time there was among certain advanced spirits a determined effort to identify—or at least confuse—Sex with love; that is, to disprove the old theological doctrine that sex took place entirely below the belt, and love entirely above it. Somewhere in the region of the heart, and if you worked at it, it could get somewhere as high as the brain. Never the twain could meet, of course, unless you were a moral acrobat, which was reprehensible. As I say, the young pioneers set out to disprove this dirty doctrine in two different directions, or schools: First, the most popular, that sex is all, just plain sex undiluted by any piffling notions about spiritual overtones, or even just a romantic glow—a good hearty low roll in the hay without getting "involved" was the best, perhaps the only, purifying thing in life....

The second school still believed in love: love that began perhaps in the heart, all tender feelings and warm hopes, worked itself up into a community of ideas, and finally got around to exploring the cellar, but only incidentally. That is to say, True Love included Sex, naturally, but it got its innings only after careful preparation in the higher

**Honoré de Balzac
(1799 – 1850)**

Balzac's love life was much like his novels: passionate and not exactly socially correct. His first love at the age of twenty-three was Madame Lare de Berney, a married woman twenty-two years his elder and the mother of nine children. After a number of affairs with English women, his next great love was Eveline Hanksa, a Polish countess married to a very wealthy, and elderly, Ukrainian land baron. Balzac delighted in cuckolding the land baron and rejoiced in his eventual death. Balzac finally married Eveline when he was fifty, just five months before his death.

departments of life. Some of these fanatics actually waited until they were married to sleep together.... Well, I noticed at last that the True Love school got divorces almost as often as the Foul Sex school, only the Foul Sexers didn't get so bruised because they had known all along that nothing lasts, while the lovers were left holding a sackful of broken ideals.

Katherine Anne Porter, *"Letters to a Nephew"*

It seems that lust, as well as overly romantic notions of love with physical delights as a dessert, are not too popular with these fine minds. So what's the best way to truly make love?

Respect your partner

One of the first important rules is to be to treat your lover like a friend and an equal rather than a sex object—or worse—a sex subject. Taoist sexual philosophy takes the concept of respect very seriously, assigning equal energies for the female "yin" and the male "yang." The flow and interplay between these male and female forces is a dynamic and ultimately energizing process, especially when both parties respect each other. This process is explained in the *Su Nu Jing,* a text written thirty-five centuries ago in China. In the book, Emperor Haungdi (also known as the Yellow Emperor) received sex advice from his advisor Su Nu, "a woman of knowledge":

A happy and harmonious sexual life depends in large measure on there being harmony and understanding between the partners.

Emperor Huangdi, *Su Nu Jing*

A key element of sexual harmony is respect, whether it is in the Eastern or Western context. Simone de Beauvoir, who was much abused in love by the cynical Sartre, has this to say about the importance of respect:

[The] battle of the sexes...can easily be solved when the woman finds in the male both desire and respect; if he lusts after her flesh while recognizing her freedom, she feels herself to be the essential, her integrity remains unimpaired the while she makes herself

Wild nights!
Wild nights!
Were I with thee,
Wild nights
should be
Our luxury!

—Emily Dickenson,
Wild Nights

object; she remains free in the submission to which she consents. Under such conditions the lovers can enjoy a common pleasure, in a fashion suitable for each, the partners each feeling the pleasure as being his or her own but as having its source in the other....

All the treasures of virility, of femininity, reflect each other, and thus they form an ever shifting and ecstatic unity. What is required for such harmony is not refinement in technique, but rather, on the foundation of the moment's erotic charm, a mutual generosity of body and soul. **Simone de Beauvoir,** *The Second Sex*

Indeed, respecting one's partner can only lead to increased sexual fulfillment for *both* partners:

It was hardly an accident that this increase in woman's sexual fulfillment accompanied her progress to equal participation in the rights, education, work, and decisions of American society. The coincidental sexual emancipation of American men—the lifting of the veil of contempt and degradation from sexual intercourse—was surely related to the American male's new regard for the American woman as equal, a person like himself, and not just a sexual object. Evidently, the further women progressed from that state, the more sex became an act of human intercourse rather than a dirty joke to men; and the more women were able to love men, rather than submit, in passive distaste, to their sexual desire. In fact, the feminine mystique itself—with its acknowledgment of woman as subject and not just object of the sexual act, and its assumption that her active, willing participation was essential to a man's pleasure—could not have come without the emancipation of women to human equality. As the early feminists foresaw, women's rights did indeed promote greater sexual fulfillment, for men and women. **Betty Friedan,** *The Feminine Mystique*

Be spontaneous

What if you respect your partner in lovemaking but the spark seems lacking? Maybe you should try something new, something unexpected. After all, making love shouldn't be like going to work; it should never become routine. (Kierkegaard reports that the Jesuits in

Paraguay found it necessary to ring a bell at midnight to remind husbands of their conjugal obligations!) Look at poor Madame Bovary. She became ineffably bored because of her husband's utterly predictable routine in lovemaking:

> *[Charles's] raptures had settled into a regular schedule; he embraced her only at certain hours. It was one habit among many, like a dessert known in advance, after a monotonous dinner.*
> **Gustave Flaubert,** *Madame Bovary*

How boring! Show some imagination: change the time, the location, the accoutrements, everything. As the good doctor says:

> *There is need of variety in sex, but not in love.*
> **Theodore Reik,** *Of Love and Lust*

After all, variety is the spice of love as well as life:

> *And yet not cloy thy lips with loath'd satiety,*
> *But rather famish them amid their plenty,*
> *Making them red and pale with fresh variety;*
> *Ten short kisses as one, one long as twenty:*
> *A summer's day will seem an hour but short,*
> *Being wasted in such time-beguiling sport.*
> **William Shakespeare,** *Venus and Adonis*

So be bold when your mood calls for it:

> *Displaying her passion*
> *In loveplay as the battle began,*
> *She launched a bold offensive*
> *Above him*
> *And triumphed over her lover.*
> *Her hips were still,*

"Love Scene," Mughal Period, early 17th century India

Her vine-like arm was slack,
Her chest was heaving,
Her eyes were closed.
Why does a mood of manly force
Succeed for women in love?

                                                              Jayadeva, *Gitagovinda*

Be generous

   With the one you love, it is not enough to be generous with your possessions but also with your acts. Thus, lovemaking is another way of showing your true nature:

The act of love, for instance, is a confession. Selfishness screams aloud, vanity shows off,
or else true generosity reveals itself.   **Albert Camus,** *The Fall*

   Remember that each little act of tenderness adds immeasurably to the entire sensual experience. We can all learn lessons from the beautiful courtesan Kamaswami, who taught the lucky Siddhartha the ways of exquisite lovemaking:

[Siddhartha] learned many things from her wise red lips. Her smooth gentle hand taught
him many things. He, who was still a boy as regards to love and was inclined to plunge
to the depths of it blindly and insatiably, was taught by her that one cannot have pleasure
without giving it, and that every gesture, every caress, every touch, every glance, every
single part of the body has its secret which can give pleasure to one who can understand.
She taught him that lovers should not separate from each other after making love without
admiring each other, with being conquered as well as conquering, so that no feeling of
satiation or desolation arises nor horrid feeling of misusing or having been misused.

                                                         Hermann Hesse, *Siddhartha*

   This generosity of the body should ideally be a gift of the self. The *Kama Sutra*, written in honor of Kama, the Hindu god of love, recognized this fact more than sixteen centuries ago:

Happiness both given and received is mutual enjoyment. For this shared happiness and pleasure, a man is willing to give himself entirely. For a man as well as a woman, the total gift of self is a source of wonderful happiness and luck. Sexual intercourse is not merely a pleasure of the senses: more important is the sacrifice of the self, the gift of self.

Vatsyayana, *Kama Sutra*

So now you've been reminded to be a thoughtful, respectful, spontaneous partner. Where does the fun come in?

Let yourself go

One of the great joys about making love is letting go of all cares and woes and just celebrating the pleasures and intimacies of your bodies. To do so, you have to leave your troubles behind and shed your shyness and modesty:

The daughter-in-law of Pythagoras said that a woman who goes to bed with a man ought to lay aside her modesty with her skirt, and put it on again with her petticoat.

Michel de Montaigne, *Essays*

When you are with a loved one, there is no need to be ashamed; rather, celebrate your togetherness:

In the short summer night she learnt so much. She would have thought that a woman would have died of shame. Instead of which, shame died. Shame, which is fear: the deep organic shame, the old, physical fear which crouches in the bodily roots of us, and can only be chased away by the sensual fire, at last it was roused up and routed by the phallic hunt of man, and she came to the very heart of the jungle herself. She felt, now, she had come to the real bedrock of her nature, and was essentially shameless. She was her sensual self, naked and unashamed. She felt a triumph, almost a vainglory. So! That was life! That was how oneself really was! There was nothing left to disguise or be ashamed of.

Everybody tells me
My hair is too long
I leave it
As I you saw it last
Dishevelled by
your hands.

—Lady Sono No
Omi Ikuha

She shared her ultimate nakedness with a man, another being.
                                            D.H. Lawrence, *Lady Chatterley's Lover*

The converse of this rule is also true: by *not* letting yourself go, you rob not only yourself of pleasure, but also your partner:

There is no pain compared to that of loving a woman who makes her body accessible to one and yet is incapable of delivering her true self—because she does not know where to find it.
                                                          Lawrence Durrell, *Justine*

Show your pleasure

Much of the joy that comes from making love is in providing your lover with great pleasure. This is partially because of our vanity: we all like to think we are great lovemakers. Thus you shouldn't be shy to show your pleasure in order to provide your partner with greater satisfaction. According to Simone de Beauvoir, it is not a matter of showing just your pleasure, but love as well. Then a woman can enjoy the entire experience as a reaffirmation of love:

[T]he act of love requires of woman profound self-abandonment; she bathes in a passive languor; with closed eyes, anonymous, lost, she feels borne by waves, swept away in a storm, shrouded in darkness: darkness of the flesh, of the womb, of the grave. Annihilated, she becomes one with the Whole, her ego is abolished. But when the man moves from her, she finds herself back on earth, on a bed, in the light; she again has a name, a face: she is one vanquished, prey, object.

This is the moment when love becomes a necessity. As when the child, after weaning, seeks the reassuring gaze of its parents, so must a woman feel, through the man's loving contemplation, that she is, after all, still at one with the Whole from which her flesh is now painfully detached. She is seldom wholly satisfied even if she has felt the orgasm, she is not completely free from the spell of her flesh; her desire continues in the form of affection. In giving her pleasure, the man increases her attachment, he does not liberate her. As for him, he no longer desires her; but she will not forgive this momentary indifference unless he has dedicated to her a timeless and absolute emotion. Then the immanence of the moment is transcended; hot memories are no regret, but a treasured delight; ebbing pleasure becomes hope and promise; enjoyment is justified; woman can gloriously accept her sexuality because she transcends it; excitement, pleasure and desire are no longer a state, but a benefaction; her body is no longer an object: it is a hymn, a flame.

Simone de Beauvoir, *The Second Sex*

Remember that much of the pleasure a lover derives is the satisfaction of the other. If there is no mutual pleasure, it is an empty game:

[Ida] slept. [Vivaldo] felt that she was sleeping partly to avoid him. He fell back on his pillow, staring up at the cracks on the ceiling. She was in his bed but she was far away from him; she was with him and yet she was not with him. In some deep, secret place she watched herself, she held herself in check, she fought him. He felt that she had decided, long ago, precisely where the limits were, how much she could afford to give, and he had not been able to make her give a penny more. She made love to him as though it was a technique of pacification, a means to some other end. However she might wish to delight him, she seemed principally to wish to exhaust him; and to remain, above all, herself on the banks of pleasure the while she labored mightily to drown him in the tide. His pleasure was enough for her, she seemed to say, his pleasure was hers. But he wanted her pleasure to be his, for them to drown in the tide together.

James Baldwin, *Another Country*

Take your time

But where is the advice on the techniques of lovemaking? Taoist sexual advice begins by emphasizing the importance of kissing and caressing as a prelude to greater delights. The *Kama Sutra* also has some hints, such as beginning slowly:

> *In approaching the spouse, or at the start when lovers unite, great precautions are necessary. The seed of desire, born of mutual attraction, must develop. To make it grow and flourish, much delicacy is needed. It must be watered with the ambrosia of kisses and caresses.*
>
> **Vatsyayana,** *Kama Sutra*

You may have to remind your lover not to get too focused on his lovemaking technique, but instead to concentrate on the whole atmosphere:

> *A man is very wrong in undertaking to impose his own rhythm or timing upon his partner and in working furiously to give her an orgasm: he would often succeed only in shattering the form of eroticism she was on the way to experiencing in her special manner.... Success does not require a mathematical synchronization of feeling, as in the oversimplified belief of many meticulous men, but the establishment of a complex erotic pattern. Many suppose that to "make" a woman feel pleasure is a matter of time and technique, indeed of violent action; they do not realize to what degree woman's sexuality is conditioned by the total situation.*
>
> **Simone de Beauvoir,** *The Second Sex*

Praise your partner

Compliments need not be confined to looks and achievements. We men also love to hear that we are admired for our skills in bed. As with any other compliments, these don't cost a penny to give and yet they can bring so much pleasure! (Just be sure to keep the praise credible.) Here is Ovid's advice for women:

> *A woman should melt with passion to her very marrow,*
> *   The act should give equal pleasure to them both:*
> *Keep up a flow of seductive whispered endearments,*

Use sexy taboo words while you're making love,
And if nature's denied you the gift of achieving a climax,
Moan as if you were coming, put on an act!...
Only take care to make your performance convincing,
Thrash about in a frenzy, roll your eyes,
Let your cries and gasping breath suggest what pleasure
You're getting....

Ovid, *The Art of Love*

Frankly, I would advise against "faking it." So does the *shunga* ("spring pleasures"), the traditional Japanese sex manual for young newlyweds. The *shunga* suggests that it's much better to gently let your partner know your pleasures. And once you *are* satisfied, be sure to say that you are sated and happy. In the memorable words of Sappho:

I am limp as
a wet worn-out dishcloth.

Sappho, *The Love Songs*

Finally, recall that *love* is the key to lovemaking, not the use of every acrobatic technique in the *Kama Sutra*. Leather outfits and other accoutrements are poor substitutes for the real thing:

Look at all these horrible little books giving advice on technical procedures and assuring
all parties that bed can be wonderful if only the subjects can get rid of their inhibitions and
practice a bag of new tricks.
Katherine Anne Porter, *"Letters to a Nephew"*

Now you have been reminded of the best ways to make love, not just to indulge in "the beast with two backs," to repeat that memorable phrase from Rabelais. Next, it's time to learn how to keep this great passion alive.

Sappho
(ca. 615 B.C. – 660 B.C.)

Sappho, the poet often called the Tenth Muse, gave us the word "sapphist" or lesbian (because she was from the island of Lesbos). Sappho supervised a school of young girls devoted to the study of poetry and the worship of Aphrodite, the Greek god of love and pleasure. Many of Sappho's poems were written in honor of her students, though she wrote love poetry celebrating both men and women. She had numerous love affairs with women and later married a man named Cercolas, who left her a widow in her forties with her daughter Cleis. She was forced to flee to Sicily for political reasons, but eventually returned to Lesbos when "her hair was white."

"Spring in Central Park," William Zorach, 1914

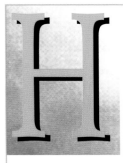

How to keep the love alive

Communicate! Let him know your needs

Allow some freedom

Don't try to "reform" him

Don't "manage" the relationship

Don't be servile

Show your affection, not your jealousy

How to keep love alive

Assuming that you've made it through the awkward Scylla and Charybdis of fantasy love and erotic love, you now have to keep that precious love alive. A good relationship is like the momentum of a bicycle; it needs to be moving forward or else it will falter. This movement requires some effort, on both sides:

No relationship in this world remains warm and close unless a real effort is made on both sides to keep it so. Human relationships, like life itself, can never remain static. They grow or diminish. But, in either case, they change. **Eleanor Roosevelt,** *You Learn by Living*

The test of a man or woman's breeding is how they behave in a quarrel.

—George Bernard Shaw, The Philanderer

Communicate! Let him know your needs

Perhaps the most important ingredient of any long-term relationship is how effectively a couple communicates with each other. Sometimes this requires a lot of talking, at other times a glance is sufficient. In any event, it is communication that conveys the basic needs and wants, which is often so different from the courting ritual:

> *However slight the terrestrial intercourse between Dante and Beatrice or Petrach and Laura, time changes the proportion of things, and in later days it is preferable to have fewer sonnets and more conversation.* **George Eliot,** *Middlemarch*

Indeed, the best part of any long-term relationship is the peculiar form of communication that springs up between two lovers:

> *The peculiar charm of marriage, which may grow irresistible to those who have once tasted it, is the duologue, the permanent conversation between two people who talk over everything and everyone till death breaks the record. It is the back-chat which, in the long run, makes a reciprocal equality more intoxicating than any form of servitude or domination.* **Cyril Connelly,** *The Unquiet Grave*

Healthy communication includes voicing grievances. Withholding your true feelings hurts you as well as your partner:

> *[Archer] was weary of living in a perpetual tepid honeymoon, without the temperature of passion yet with all of its exactions. If [his wife] had spoken out her grievances (he suspected her of many) he might have laughed them away; but she was trained to conceal imaginary wounds under a Spartan smile.* **Edith Wharton,** *The Age of Innocence*

Allow some freedom

In any healthy relationship, both partners need to allow the other a chance to grow and expand on his or her own. This means letting go sometimes, even when this seems difficult:

Love does not cause suffering; what causes it is the sense of ownership, which is love's opposite.

Antoine de Saint-Exupéry, *The Wisdom of the Sands*

Above all, you do not want to suffocate your budding love. Give your relationship a chance to breathe:

Artists misunderstand love.... They believe they are selfless in love because they desire the advantage of another being, often to the prejudice of their own advantage. But in exchange they want to possess that other being....

Friedrich Nietzsche, *The Wagner Case*

The best way to look at this issue is in the positive sense of enlarging love for both parties:

For this is to blame, if anything is:
not to multiply the freedom of a love
with all the freedom that one can bring forth.
We need, when we love, really only this:
to let each other go; for holding on
is easy and does not have to be learned.

Rainer Maria Rilke, *Requiem*

No doubt you noticed that the writers who declared the necessity of freedom are men. This reflects the fact that we men occasionally need to create our own space and be on our own for a while. This does not mean we are rejecting our mates; we just want to sort things out on our own. Whether or not you totally understand this masculine impulse, please remember that this sense of freedom is important to men:

Vronsky appreciated this desire not only to please but to serve him, which had become the sole aim of [Anna's] existence, but at the same time he chafed at the loving snares in which she tried to hold him fast. As time went on, and he saw himself further and further caught in these meshes, the more he longed not so much to escape from them as to try whether

Leo Tolstoy
(1828 – 1910)

The author of Anna Karenina *and* War and Peace *was an untamed rake in his young soldiering days in the Crimea, frequenting both brothels and bars. After his military experiences, he unsuccessfully courted Valeria Arsenev, a charming though superficial girl. In 1862, at the age of thirty-two, he married Sonya (Sofya) Andreyevna Bers, a middle-class woman much younger than he. During their engagement, Tolstoy showed her his diary that included accounts of his carousing days with prostitutes, which obviously horrified the chaste Sonya. They had a tempestuous half-century marriage that produced many children. At the age of eighty-two, Tolstoy left home in a fit of rage at his wife, and he died alone at a remote railway station.*

they interfered with his freedom. Had it not been for this ever-increasing desire to be free, not to have a scene every time he had to absent himself from home for the sessions or the races, Vronsky would have been quite content with his life.　**Leo Tolstoy**, *Anna Karenina*

Finally, it is helpful to remember that a little absence may be healthy for a relationship:

The joy of life is variety; the tenderest love requires to be rekindled by intervals of absence.
Samuel Johnson, *The Idler*

Don't try to "reform" him

Let's assume you're communicating brilliantly and giving him a little space (and keeping some for yourself) when he needs to be on his own. But there are still a few things about your true love that drive you crazy and you want to relieve him of these bad habits. Although you may think this is a generous impulse on your part, Henry Fielding is hardly sympathetic:

There is perhaps no surer mark of folly than to attempt to correct natural infirmities of those we love.
Henry Fielding, *Tom Jones*

This instinct is cruelly skewered by Camus by his confessional protagonist in *The Fall*:

Our feminine friends have in common with Bonaparte the belief that they can succeed where everyone has failed.
Albert Camus, *The Fall*

Even Oscar Wilde can't resist teasing about this impulse. The poor man was subjected to numerous attempts to reform his wandering ways, not only by his wife, Constance Lloyd, but by several other well-meaning women. With his outrageous wit, he could not help lampooning this noble sentiment in his first successful play, *Lady Windermere's Fan*:

Cecil Graham: *You'll play [cards], of course, Tuppy?*

Lord Augustus: (pouring himself out a brandy and soda on the table) Can't, dear boy. Promised Mrs. Erlynne never to play or drink again.

Cecil Graham: Now, my dear Tuppy, don't be led astray into the paths of virtue. Reformed, you would be perfectly tedious. That is the worst of women. They always want one to be good. And if we are good, they don't love us at all. They like to find us quite irretrievably bad, and leave us quite unattractively good.

Lord Darlington: They always do find us bad!

Dumby: I don't think we are bad. I think we are all good except Tuppy.

Lord Darlington: No, we are all in the gutter, but some of us are looking at the stars.

Oscar Wilde, *Lady Windermere's Fan*

Another reason to overcome the need to reform the man you love is simple pragmatism. After all, who knows how effective your efforts will be at changing your lover from his lifelong habits? As the old aphorism from Zaire goes:

Wood may remain ten years in the water, but it will never become a crocodile.

Proverb from Zaire

Worst of all, some unscrupulous men are more than ready to take advantage of this generous, but counterproductive, impulse on the part of women who want to "change" them. Note the slimy Svidrigailov's confession about his seduction of a good-hearted woman:

When a girl starts pitying—watch out, she's in danger. She starts wanting to "save" you and bring you to reason; revive you and recall you to more decent goals; restore you to a new life and new work—I guess you know the sort of thing they can dream up. I saw immediately that the little bird was flying straight into the net; so, for my part, I got ready.

Fyodor Dostoyevsky, *Crime and Punishment*

Don't "manage" the relationship

Another impulse to resist (if indeed you are tempted) is the impulse to "manage" the relationship. By all means, calmly convey your needs and desires. Just don't micro-manage:

A whole tradition enjoins upon wives the art of "managing" a man; one must discover and humor his weaknesses and must cleverly apply in due measure flattery and scorn, docility and resistance, vigilance and leniency. This last mixture of attitudes is an especially delicate matter. A husband must be granted neither too much or too little freedom. If she is too obliging, a wife finds her husband escaping her; and she runs the risk of having a mistress get enough power over him to make him divorce her or at least to take first place in his life. But if she denies him any adventures whatever, if she annoys him with her watchfulness, her scenes, her demands, she is likely to turn him definitely against her. It is a matter of knowing how to "make concessions" designedly; if one's husband "cheats" a little, one will close one's eyes; but at other times one must keep them wide open....

This is indeed a melancholy science—to dissimulate, to use trickery, to hate and fear in silence, to play on the vanity and weaknesses of a man, to learn to thwart him, to deceive him, to "manage" him.

Simone de Beauvoir, *The Second Sex*

The real problem with this type of management is that it tends to strangle the love you are trying to retain:

Leonora could not be aware that the man whom she loved passionately and whom, nevertheless, she was beginning to try to rule with a rod of iron—that this man was becoming more and more estranged from her. He seemed to regard her as being not only physically and mentally cold, but even as being actually wicked and mean.... She could not see that in trying to curb what she regarded as megalomania she was doing anything wicked. She was just trying to keep things together for the sake of the children who did not come. And, little by little, the whole of their intercourse became simply one of agonized discussion....

Ford Madox Ford, *The Good Soldier*

Don't be servile

On the other hand, you can't let a man take advantage of your kindness either. Unfortunately, too much kindness can be taken for servility, which often breeds contempt. Encourage him do his fair share of the housework, lest your labors be taken for granted. Take for example the detestable treatment of Charles Bovary's mother by his father in Flaubert's *Madame Bovary*:

His wife had been mad about him in the beginning; she had loved him with a boundless servility that made him even more indifferent to her. She had been vivacious, expansive and brimming over with affection in her youth, but as she became older she became peevish, nagging and nervous, like sour wine turning to vinegar. She had suffered so much at first without complaining, watching him run after every village strumpet in sight and having him come home to her every night, satiated and stinking of alcohol, after carousing in a score of ill-famed establishments! Then her pride rebelled; she withdrew into herself, swallowing her rage with a mute stoicism which she maintained until her death. She was always busy with domestic and financial matters. She was constantly going to see lawyers or the judge, remembering when notes were due and obtaining renewals; and at home she spent all her time ironing, sewing, washing, supervising the workmen and settling the itemized bills they presented to her, while Monsieur, totally unconcerned with everything and continually sinking into a sullen drowsiness from which he roused himself only to make disagreeable remarks to her, sat smoking beside the fire and spitting into the ashes.

Gustave Flaubert, *Madame Bovary*

Let your love be like the misty rain, coming softly, but flooding the river.

—Proverb from Madagascar

Likewise, you should never beg your man to do or not do something; this is demeaning to you and will not change the long-term outcome. In this pitiful scene from Virgil's *The Aeneid*, Dido, the Queen of Carthage, pleads with her lover, Aeneas, not to leave her for his obligations in Italy:

Do you go to get away from me? I beg you,
By these tears, by your own right hand, since I
Have left my wretched self nothing but that—
Yes, by the marriage we entered on,
If ever I did well and you were grateful
Or found some sweetness in a gift from me,
Have pity now on a declining house!
Put this plan by, I beg you, if a prayer
Is not yet out of place.

Virgil, *The Aeneid*

Despite such desperate entreaties, Aeneas left anyway. The moral of the story: it doesn't pay to beg!

Show your affection

Once a relationship has begun and some of the delicacies of the initial stages are overcome, then it becomes not just desirable but necessary to show some affection, if only to unburden your heart and to delight your lover:

Just make us believe we're loved—a simple
Assignment: desire is quick to kindle faith
In what it seeks.

Ovid, *The Art of Love*

...not your jealousy

Certainly, jealousy is not the sole preserve of women, but if it is exhibited too often on the part of either partner it can be a powerful deterrent to forming a relationship based on trust. With perhaps some exaggeration, Simone de Beauvoir documents this sad passion:

The woman in love, suspicious and mistaken in turn, is obsessed by the desire to discover the fatal truth and the fear that she will.... Woman rarely consents to ask herself the question: does he really love me? but she asks herself a hundred times: does he love someone else? She does not admit that the fervor of her lover can have died down little by little, nor that he values love less than she does: she immediately invents rivals.... In a state of uncertainty, every woman is a rival, a danger. **Simone de Beauvoir,** *The Second Sex*

This passion is illustrated perfectly by Tolstoy, whose experience with a jealous wife gave him ample material to draw on for his masterpiece *Anna Karenina.* (In defense of his wife, Sonya, Tolstoy gave her more than enough reason to be jealous.) We can see Anna Karenina's growing jealousy toward her lover, Count Vronsky, not long before her suicide:

In her eyes Vronsky, with all his habits, ideas, desires—his whole spiritual and physical temperament could be summed up in one thing—love for women, and this love, which she felt ought to be wholly concentrated on her, was diminishing. Therefore, she reasoned, he must have transferred part of it to other women, or to another woman, and she was jealous. She was jealous not of any particular woman but of his love. Not having yet an object for her jealousy, she was on the look-out for one. At the slightest provocation she transferred her jealousy from one object to another. Now she was jealous of the low amours he might so easily enter into through his bachelor connections; now it was the society women he might meet; now she was jealous of some imaginary girl whom he might want to marry and for whose sake he would break with her.

The result, of course, is that Vronsky begins to rebel against Anna's jealousy:

These fits of jealousy, which of late had been more and more frequent, horrified him and, however much he tried to disguise the fact, estranged him from her, although he knew the cause of her jealousy was her love for him. How often he had told himself that to be loved by her was happiness; and now that she loved him as only a woman can love for whom love outweighs all that is good in life, he was much farther from happiness than when he followed her from Moscow. Then he had considered himself unhappy, but happiness was before him; now he felt that his best happiness was behind him.

Leo Tolstoy, *Anna Karenina*

Blind jealousy also leads to the tedium of repeating the same old questions and answers, with the answers becoming less and less in accordance with the truth:

[The woman in love] compels the man to lie to her: "Do you love me? As much as yesterday? Will you always love me?" and so on. She cleverly poses her questions at a moment when there is not time enough to give properly qualified and sincere answers, or more especially when circumstances prevent any response; she asks insistent questions in the course of a sexual embrace, at the verge of a convalescence, in the midst of sobs, or on a railroad platform. She makes trophies of the extorted replies; if there are no replies, she takes silence to mean what she wishes.... **Simone de Beauvoir,** *The Second Sex*

On the other hand, if your man is too jealous of *you* and is driving you crazy, inform him in no uncertain terms that this attitude is killing your love:

Jealousy: that dragon which slays love under the pretense of keeping it alive.

Havelock Ellis, *On Life and Sex*

Tell him that the sad consequence of too much jealous anxiety is that it kills the very love it is trying so desperately to hold:

Anxiety is love's greatest killer, because it is like the stranglehold of the drowning.

Anaïs Nin, *The Diary of Anaïs Nin*

It may seem after this litany of "don'ts" that I have placed the onus for a healthy relationship on women, but trust me, our panel of love experts has assigned plenty of responsibilities for men as well. That important topic is handled in my next book, *Love Advice for Men,* which explains what men can do to help keep love alive. (Hint: part of the advice to men involves staying faithful and doing their fair share of the domestic work.) However, in the unfortunate event that the two of you are not able to keep your love alive, let's take a look at the cures to ease a breaking heart.

Anaïs Nin
(1903 – 1977)

The internationally famous writer of erotic diaries and novels, Nin was born in Paris of Spanish-French-Danish heritage. She moved to the United States as a young girl and began writing intimate diaries at the age of sixteen. Around age twenty, she married Hugh (Hugo) Guiler, a complaisant banker who worshipped her all his life. They moved from New York to Paris in 1925, where she started keeping two sets of diaries: a false one for her husband to read and a "real" diary filled with the details of her numerous love affairs, including Henry Miller, Otto Rank and Edmund Wilson. Eventually, she and Hugo moved back to New York, where she started an affair with Rupert Pole, a man sixteen years younger than she. Pole was a failed actor who eventually moved back to his home in southern California. Not willing to give up the handsome Rupert or to divorce her compliant husband, she eventually married Rupert in 1955, falsely telling him that she had divorced Hugo. She maintained a precarious bicoastal relationship with both men for twenty-two years until she died.

Cures for love

Keep busy with work

Spend time with friends

Don't over-analyze your love woes

Concentrate on the flaws of the beloved

Get sick of fantasy love

Show some pride

Opt for a friendly separation

Remember that time heals all wounds

Be open to new relationships

Left: "Luncheon of the Boating Party," Pierre Auguste Renoir, 1881

Cures for Love

Alas, it didn't work out. All your carefully nurtured dreams, formulated in many a feverish night of tossing and turning in bed, have been dashed. Perhaps you have reason to complain to Antieros, the god of unrequited love. But take heart; there's some effective medicine at hand. Not that anything is perfect, of course:

> *There are several cures for love, but none of them is infallible.*
> **François, duc de La Rochefoucauld,** *Maxim 459*

Let's put this painful period in perspective. It doesn't sound like much consolation now, but Tennyson's old line that "'Tis better to have loved and lost/Than never to have loved at all" has some validity. More eloquently, Katherine Anne Porter emphasizes the positive aspects of having experienced a relationship that has gone bad by emphasizing the "brief shining moment" when the behavior of human beings is at their best:

> *And when it is over, it is over. And when I have recovered from the shock, and sorted out the damage and put my mangled life in order, I can then begin to remember what really happened. It is probably the silliest kind of love there is, but I'm glad I had it. I'm glad there were times when I saw human beings at their best, for I don't think by any means that I lent them all their radiance...it was there ready to be brought out by someone who loved them. It is still there, it may have shone out again if they were ever loved like that again. It is just that I knew them better than anyone else for a little while, they showed me a different face because they knew I could really see it—and no matter what came of it, I remember and never deny what I saw.* **Katherine Anne Porter,** *"Letters to a Nephew"*

Keep busy with work

We can recognize that there were some good moments, but right now we need all the help we can get, especially from Ovid, who is one of our key apothecaries for cures on love. He literally wrote the book on *Cures for Love* and he remains my number one source two thousand years later. His regimen is strict—like all good rehabilitation techniques—but effective. Ovid's first rule is to keep busy:

> No leisure—that's rule
> Number one. Leisure stimulates love, leisure watches the lovelorn,
> Leisure's the cause and sustenance of this sweet
> Evil. Eliminate leisure, and Cupid's bow is broken,
> His torches lie lightless, scorned.
> As a plane-tree rejoices in wine, as a poplar in water,
> As a marsh-reed in swampy ground, so Venus loves
> Leisure: if you want an end to your loving, keep busy—
> Love gives way to business—and you'll be safe.
> Listlessness, too much sleep (no morning appointments), nights at
> The gambling tables, or on the bottle—these
> Inflict no wounds, yet ruin your moral fiber, open
> A way for insidious Love to breach your heart.
> Cupid homes in on sloth, detests the active—so give that
> Bored mind of yours some really absorbing work....

Ovid, *Cures for Love*

Spend time with friends

Thus far you've managed to keep busy at work all day without dwelling too much on your tragic loss. Now what? Should you go home and burrow into some triple fudge concoction? Of course not! It's much better to surround yourself with your friends or acquaintances. That's what friends are for:

> Friendship is certainly the finest balm for the pangs of disappointed love.

Jane Austen, *Northanger Abbey*

Let your friends cheer you up. After all, it could be a lot worse—just think of how much

---

Absence, that common cure of love.

—Miguel de Cervantes, Don Quixote de la Mancha

worse if the break-up had occurred later:

Have you no comforts? No friends? Is your loss such as leaves no opening for consolation? Much as you suffer now, think of what you would have suffered if the discovery of his character had been delayed to a later period, if your engagement had been carried on for months and months, as it might have been, before he chose to put an end to it. Every additional day of unhappy confidence on your side would have made the blow more dreadful.

Jane Austen, *Sense and Sensibility*

Now is the time to organize some activities with your friends. The primary strategy during this difficult period is to stay in the presence of other people:

Lonely places, you lovers, are dangerous: shun lonely places,
    Don't opt out, you'll be safer in a crowd!
You've no need for secrecy (secrecy fosters passion):
    From now on, company's what you need.
If you're solitary, you'll be sad, your forsaken mistress
    Always there in your mind's eye,
A too vivid presence. That's why night's grimmer than daytime:
The friends who might relieve your mood aren't there.
    Don't avoid conversation, don't shut the door on callers,
Don't hide yourself away and cry in the dark.
    Always have some Pylades there to back up Orestes[1]:
Of friendship's various benefits, this
    Is by no means the slightest.

Ovid, *Cures for Love*

Don't over-analyze your love woes

Sometimes it is best not to analyze endlessly about your woes; endless rehashing of the same issues actually may be counterproductive. As the old French proverb warns, "Try to reason about love and you will lose your reason."

---

[1] Faithful friends depicted in *The Libation Bearers* by Aeschylus.

Marcel Proust thinks that love is closer to delusion than to reason and therefore its demise defies logical analysis:

However, with every occurrence in life and its contrasting situations that relate to love, it is best to make no attempt to understand, since insofar as these are as inexorable as they are unlooked-for, they appear to be governed by magic rather than by rational laws....

Marcel Proust, *Within a Budding Grove*

Concentrate on the flaws of the beloved

Thus far you've been a saint. You've thrown yourself into work and worthwhile social activities. You've avoided the cheap temptations or temporary pleasures that change nothing. But we are human after all, and subject to some of the bittersweet joys of revenge— even if they are Pyrrhic and short-lived. Why not just concentrate, for a moment, on the shortcomings of your erstwhile lover? Perhaps it wasn't such a great love after all! Listen to poor Titania confessing her distress to a friend over a love no longer felt:

My Oberon, what visions I have seen!
Methought I was enamored of an ass.

William Shakespeare, *A Midsummer's Night Dream*

Sei Shonagon suggests cutting to the heart of the matter: seriously question your ex-lover's ability to really be a loving man:

When a woman runs into a lover with whom (alas!) she has broken for good, there is no reason for her to be ashamed if he regards her as heartless. But if the lover shows that he has not even been even slightly upset by their parting, which to her was so sad and painful and difficult, she is bound to be amazed by the man and to wonder what sort of a heart he can have.

Sei Shonagon, *The Pillow Book*

If you're truly successful in denigrating your ex-lover in your mind, you'll wonder

Sei Shonagon (ca. 965 – 1005)

The precursor of the Japanese genre known as zuihitsu ("random notes") was a lady-in-waiting to Empress Sadako. She wrote about her observations of the social and sexual mores of the Imperial Court in The Pillow Book. *She reputedly married a government official named Tachibana no Norimitsu and possibly had a son.*

why you ever were interested in the first place:

> *When one has stopped loving somebody, one feels that he has become someone else, even*
> *though he is still the same person.*   **Sei Shonagon,** *The Pillow Book*

Get sick of fantasy love

Sometimes it also helps to be (temporarily) sick of fantasy love as well as of the lover. Sor Juana, the famous Muse of Mexico, laments the passing of her love with the liberating philosophy of feeling there is nothing left to lose:

> *Disillusionment,*
> *this is the bitter end,*
> *this proves you're rightly called*
> *the end of illusion.*
> *You've made me lose all,*
> *yet no, losing all*
> *is not paying too dear*
> *for being undeceived.*
> *No more will you envy*
> *the allurements of love,*
> *for one undeceived*
> *has no risk left to run.*
> *It's some consolation*
> *to be expecting none:*
> *there's relief to be found*
> *in seeking no cure.*
> *In loss itself*
> *I find assuagement:*
> *having lost the treasure,*
> *I've nothing to fear.*

Having nothing to lose
brings peace of mind:
one traveling without funds
need not fear thieves....   **Sor Juana,** *Poem 7*

For friends dealing with the heartbroken, the key is to listen to their love woes, and hold back from offering similar experiences or horror stories. Nor should you try to find a silver lining or change the topic. The subject will rise again anyway, so you might as well let your suffering friend talk it out of her system. Stendhal, ever compassionate to those suffering in love, offers this suggestion for succoring friends:

Far from seeking crudely and openly to distract the lover, the healing friend should rather
talk to him ad nauseam *about this love and his mistress, and at the same time contrive a*
whole succession of trivial happenings around him.   **Stendhal,** *On Love*

Show some pride

Exhibiting a little pride is also necessary. Begging for a lover to come back is a loser's game. After all:

The sufferings of love should ennoble, not degrade. Pride is of some use in love.
                                                       George Sand, *Intimate Journal*

Indeed, pride is sometimes the only way to get you through the first few days without collapsing:

Pride and reserve are not the only things in life; perhaps they are not even the best things.
But if they happen to be your particular virtues you will go all to pieces if you let them go.
                                                       Ford Madox Ford, *The Good Soldier*

Feigning indifference will require some acting, though, as professor Ovid points out:

Why should I be bitter
About someone who was
A complete stranger
Until a certain moment
In a day that has passed.

—Saigyo

When you feel like crying, laugh.
(I'm not saying jettison your passion
In mid-course: my regimen is not that harsh.)
Simulate what you are not, pretend the fit's abated—
Faking it will lead to the genuine thing.   **Ovid,** *Cures for Love*

Opt for a friendly separation

But don't let this coolness turn into hatred. Nothing is more self-destructive or energy-consuming than lapsing into bitterness against your erstwhile lover. After all, hatred always corrodes the container. As hard as it may seem in these bitter moments, it is always more noble to resist the temptation to insult what you once loved:

How natural it is to destroy what we cannot possess, to deny what we do not understand,
and to insult what we envy.   **Honoré de Balzac**

This advice raises the delicate issue of whether or not you should stay friends with an "ex." The best answer is not to resume social contact until you are completely cured:

Many of us marvel at the icy insensitivity with which women snuff out their amours. But
if they did not blot out the past in this manner, life for them would lose all dignity and they
could never resist the fatal familiarities to which they once submitted.   **Honoré de Balzac**

Frankly speaking, it is difficult—if not impossible— to return to the old ways of emotional intimacy after a break-up and to become "just friends":

Oh, there once was a lady, and so I've been told,
Whose lover grew weary, whose lover grew cold
"My child," he remarked, "though our episode ends,
In the manner of men, I suggest we be friends."

And the truest of friends after they were—
Oh, they lied through their teeth when they told me of her!

Dorothy Parker, *"Fable"*

Remember that time heals most wounds

It is helpful to remember that no matter how awful the present seems, the passage of time eventually will heal most, if not all, of the scars:

It is time, not the mind, that puts an end to love.   **Publilius Syrus,** *Maxims*

Don't expect the healing process to work instantly. Alas, the deeper the wound, the more time it takes to heal:

In the multiple peregrinations of love, Sabina was quick to recognize the echoes of larger loves and desires. The large ones, particularly if they had not died a natural death, never died completely and left reverberations. Once interrupted, broken artificially, suffocated accidentally, they continued to exist in separate fragments and endless smaller echoes.

A vague physical resemblance, an almost similar mouth, a slightly similar voice, some particle of the character of Philip, or John, would emigrate to another, whom she recognized immediately in a crowd, at a party, by the erotic resonance it reawakened.

The echoes struck at first through the mysterious instrumentation of the senses which retained sensations as instruments retain a sound after being touched. The body remained vulnerable to certain repetitions long after the mind believed it made a clear, final severance.   **Anaïs Nin,** *A Spy in the House of Love*

Ovid suggests no harsh remedies; let the passage of time work its healing magic:

Don't attempt to extinguish your ardour
At a stroke, but by slow degrees: phase it out
And you'll be quite safe. Flash floods run deeper than a perennial
River, but are soon gone: the river flows
All year through. Let love wane in slow evanescence,
Fade on the breeze and die.
                                                    Ovid, *Cures for Love*

Don't despair—sometimes the scars can heal more rapidly. Dorothy Parker suggests that it takes all of six months to be completely cured:

In May my heart was breaking—
  Oh, wide the wound, and deep!
And bitter it beat at waking,
  And sore it split in sleep.

And when it came to November,
  I sought my heart, and sighed,
"Poor thing, do you remember?"
  "What heart was that?" it cried.
                                    Dorothy Parker,*"Autumn Valentine"*

Be open to new relationships

While it is important to give some time to properly grieve the end of a relationship, now is not the time to bitterly renounce the possibility of a successful love in the future. Indeed, many relationships start when they are least expected:

When the heart is still shaken by the remains of a passion we are more likely to yield to
a fresh one than when we are quite cured.
                        François, duc de La Rochefoucauld, *Maxim 484*

Although we cannot dictate our fate in love, we *do* have the power to determine our attitude toward loving again. In this vein, Proust suggests keeping an open mind about the possibilities of a new relationship:

> *We scornfully decline [an invitation to meet another potential date], because of one whom we love and who will one day be of so little account, to see another who is of no importance today, whom we shall love tomorrow, whom we might perhaps, had we consented to see her now, have loved a little sooner and who would thus have put a term to our present sufferings, bringing others, it is true, in their place.*
>
> **Marcel Proust,** *Within a Budding Grove*

When you feel that you have sufficiently mourned your lost love and are ready to move on, then it is time to start taking the tentative first steps toward a new relationship. Take the advice of Pandarus to the heartbroken Troilus:

> *As Zanzis in his wisdom said, moreover,*
> *"The new love often chases out the old."*
> *New cases call for new considerations.*
> *Remember, too, you owe your life a duty.*
>
> **Geoffrey Chaucer,** *Troilus and Cressida*

So take heart! With a little luck and skill you can develop a more solid foundation for your next love relationship and hopefully you won't need to take the "cure." Remember that there are plenty of models of happy couples: Abraham and Sarah, Jacob and Rachel, Boris and Natasha, to name but a few. And perhaps someday you can say to yourself Virgil's words (if you are inclined to Latin): *Agnosco veleris vestigia flammae,* or, "I feel anew that spark of the old flame."

ART ACKNOWLEDGMENTS

Grateful acknowledgment is made to the museums for permission to reproduce the artwork listed below:

Thomas Hart Benton
Romance, 1931 – 32
Jack S. Blanton Museum of Art,
The University of Texas at Austin
Gift of Mari and James A. Michener, 1991.
Photo Credit: George Holmes

Jennie Augusta Brownscombe
(American, 1850 – 1936)
Love's Young Dream, 1887, Oil on canvas,
21-1/4 x 32-1/8 in., detail
The National Museum of Women in the Arts,
Washington, D.C.
Gift of Wallace and Wilhelmina Holladay

Marc Chagall
The Dream, 1939
The Phillips Collection, Washington, D.C.

Camille Claudel
La Valse (The Waltz), S. 1013, bronze
Musee Rodin, Paris
Photographed by Bruno Jarret
©1999 Artists Rights Society (ARS), New York/
ADAGP, Paris

Gustav Klimt
Der Kuss (The Kiss), detail
Österreichische Galerie Belveder, Vienna

Love Scene. India, Mughal period, early 17th
century. Color on paper, 26 x 17.9 cm.
©The Cleveland Museum of Art, 1998,
James Parmelee and Cornelia Blakemore Warner
Funds, 1968.107

Lovers (Mithuna). India, Madyha Pradesh,
Khajuraho style, 11th century. Reddish sandstone,
H. 74 cm.
©The Cleveland Museum of Art, 1988,
Leonard C. Hanna, Jr., Fund, 1982.64

Bartolome Esteban Murillo
Two Women at a Window, c. 1655/1660,
oil on canvas, Widener Collection
©1998 Board of Trustees,
National Gallery of Art, Washington, D.C.

*Pair Statue of Mycerinus
and Queen Kha-merer-nebty II*
11.1738
Egypt, Dynasty IV, Giza,
Valley Temple of Mycerinus
Greywacke
H: 54 ´ in. (1.39 m)
Base: 57 x 54 cm
Museum of Fine Arts, Boston
Harvard-Museum Expedition

Pierre Auguste Renoir
The Luncheon of the Boating Party, 1881
The Phillips Collection, Washington, D.C.

Titian
Venus and Adonis, 1560,
oil on canvas, Widener Collection
©1998 Board of Trustees,
National Gallery of Art, Washington, D.C.

Henri de Toulouse-Lautrec
Quadrille at the Moulin Rouge, 1892, Photograph
Chester Dale Collection
©1998 Board of Trustees,
National Gallery of Art, Washington, D.C.

William Zorach
Spring in Central Park, 1914, Painting. American.
The Metropolitan Museum of Art,
Anonymous Gift, 1979. (1979.223)
Photograph
©1979 The Metropolitan Museum of Art,
New York

QUOTATION ACKNOWLEDGMENTS

Grateful acknowledgment is made to the publishers and rights holders for permission to reprint the quotations from the authors listed below:

Achebe, Chinua. From ANTHILLS OF THE SAVANNAH by Chinua Achebe. Copyright © 1987 by Chinua Achebe. Used by permission of Doubleday, a division of Random House, Inc. From A MAN OF THE PEOPLE by Chinua Achebe. Copyright ©1966, renewed 1994 by Chinua Achebe. Used by permission of Harper Collins Publishers, Inc.

Baldwin, James. Exerpted from ANOTHER COUNTRY ©1960, 1962 by James Baldwin. Copyright renewed. Published by Vintage Books. Reprinted by permission.

Balzac, Honoré de. Reprinted with the permission of Peter Pauper Press, Inc. from EPIGRAMS ON MEN, WOMEN AND LOVE. Copyright © 1959 by Peter Pauper Press, Inc.

Beauvoir, Simone de. From THE SECOND SEX by Simone de Beauvoir. Copyright ©1952 and renewed 1980 by Alfred A. Knopf, Inc. Reprinted by permission of Alfred A. Knopf, Inc.

Camus, Albert. From THE FALL by Albert Camus. Translated by Justin O'Brian. Copyright ©1956 by Alfred A. Knopf, Inc. Reprinted by permission of Alfred A. Knopf, Inc.

Chaucer, Geoffrey. From THE PORTABLE CHAUCER by Theodore Morrison. Copyright ©1949, © 1975, renewed ©1977 by Theodore Morrison. Used by permission of Viking Penguin, a division of Penguin Putnam Inc.

Chekhov, Anton. From THE PORTABLE CHEKHOV by Anton Chekhov, edited by Avrahm Yarmolinsky. Copyright ©1947, ©1968 by Viking Penguin, Inc. Renewed by Avrahm Yarmolinsky. Used by permission of Viking Penguin, a division of Penguin Putnam Inc.

Connelly, Cyril. Selections from THE UNQUIET GRAVE: A WORD CYCLE by Palinurus (Cyril Connelly). Copyright ©1981 by Dierdre Levi. Reprinted by permission of Persea Books, Inc.

Dostoyevsky, Fyodor. From CRIME AND PUNISHMENT by Fyodor Dostoyevsky, translated by Sidney Monas. Copyright ©1968 by Sidney Monas. Used by permission of Dutton Signet, a division of Penguin Putnam Inc.

Durrell, Lawrence. From JUSTINE by Lawrence Durrell. Copyright ©1957, by Lawrence Durrell. Used by permission of Penguin Putnam Inc.

Flaubert, Gustave. "Excerpts," from MADAME BOVARY by Gustave Flaubert, translated by Lowell Blair, translation copyright ©1959 by Bantam, a division of Bantam Doubleday Dell Publishing Group, Inc. Used by permission of Bantam Books, a division of Random House, Inc.

Friedan, Betty. From THE FEMININE MYSTIQUE by Betty Friedan. Copyright ©1983, 1974, 1973, 1963 by Betty Friedan. Reprinted by permission of W. W. Norton & Company, Inc.

Fromm, Erich. From THE ART OF LOVING by Erich Fromm. Copyright ©1956 by Erich Fromm. Copyright renewed ©1984 by Annis Fromm. Reprinted by permission of Harper Collins Publishers, Inc.

Goethe, Johann Wolfgang von. From FAUST by Johann Wolfgang von Goeth, translated by Peter Salm, Translation copyright ©1985 by Peter Salm. Used by permission of Bantam Books, a division of Random House, Inc. From ELECTIVE AFFINITIES by Johann Wolfgang von Goethe, translated by R.J. Hollingdale (Penguin Classics, 1971). Translation copyright © R.J.

Hollingdale, 1971. Reproduced by permission of Penguin Books, Ltd.

Gracián, Balthasar. From THE ART OF WORLDLY WISDOM by Balthasar Gracian translated by Joseph Jacobs. ©1993 by Shambhala Publications, Inc. Boston.

Hurston, Zora Neale. From THEIR EYES WERE WATCHING GOD by Zora Neale Hurston. Copyright ©1937 by Harper & Row, Publishers, Inc. Renewed 1965 by John C. Hurston and Joel Hurston. Reprinted by permission of HarperCollins Publishers, Inc.

Jayadeva. From LOVE SONG OF THE DARK LORD, edited by Barbara Stoler Miller. Copyright ©1977 Columbia University Press. Reprinted with the permission of the publisher.

Jung, Carl. Jung, Carl Gustav: THE PORTABLE JUNG. Copyright ©1971 by Princeton University Press. Reprinted by permission of Princeton University Press.

Kierkegaard, Søren. A KIERKEGAARD ANTHOLOGY. Copyright ©1946 by Princeton University Press. Reprinted by permission of Princeton University Press. Renewed 1974.

Laclos, Choderlos de. From LES LIASIONS DANGEREUSES by Choderlos de Laclos, translated by P.W.K. Stone (Penguin Classics, 1961) copyright © P.W.K. Stone, 1961. Reproduced by permission of Penguin Books, Ltd.

McCullers, Carson. Excerpt from "The Ballad of the Sad Café," from THE BALLAD OF THE SAD CAFE AND COLLECTED SHORT STORIES by Carson McCullers. Copyright ©1936,1941,1942, 1950, ©1955 by Carson McCullers. Copyright ©1979 by Floria V. Lasky. Reprinted by permission of Houghton Mifflin Company. All rights reserved.

Montaigne, Michel de. From ESSAYS by Michel de Montaigne, translated by J.M. Cohen (Penguin Classics, 1958) copyright © J.M. Cohen, 1958. Reproduced by permission of Penguin Books, Ltd.

Murasaki Shikibu, Lady. From TALE OF GENJI by Lady Murasaki Shikibu. Translated by Edward G. Seidensticker. Copyright ©1976 by Edward G. Seidensticker. Reprinted by permission of Alfred A. Knopf, Inc.

Nietzche, Friedrich. From A NIETZSCHE READER by Fredrich Nietzsche, selected and translated by R.J. Hollingdale (Penguin Classics, 1977) Selection and translation copyright © R.J. Hollingdale, 1977. Reproduced by permission of Penguin Books, Ltd.

Nin, Anaïs. From A SPY IN THE HOUSE OF LOVE, by Anaïs Nin. Copyright ©1954, 1959, 1974 by Anaïs Nin. Copyright ©1982 by The Anaïs Nin Trust. All rights reserved. Reprinted by permission of the author's representative Gunther Stuhlman.

Ortega y Gasset, José. From TREASURY OF SPANISH LOVE translated by Juan and Susan Serrano. Copyright ©1995 by Hippocrene Books. Reprinted by permission of Hippocrene Books.

Otomo No Sakanoe, Lady. "You Say I Will Come," from ONE HUNDRED POEMS FROM THE JAPANESE by Kenneth Rexroth. Copyright © All Rights Reserved by New Directions Publishing Corporation. Reprinted by permission of New Directions Publishing Corporation.

Ovid. From THE EROTIC POEMS by Ovid, translated by Peter Green (Penguin Classics, 1982) copyright © Peter Green, 1982. Reproduced by permission of Penguin Books, Ltd.

Parker, Dorothy. "Fair Weather," copyright 1928, renewed ©1956 by Dorothy Parker, "General Review of the Sex Situation,"copyright 1926, renewed ©1954 by Dorothy Parker, "Indian Summer," copyright 1926, renewed ©1954 by

INDEX OF AUTHORS AND PAINTERS

QUICK ORDER FORM

Fax orders: Send this form to (732) 225-1562.
Telephone orders: Call 1 (800) 210-ZONE toll free. Please have your credit card ready.
Website orders: Visit *www.advicezone.com* for a secure server order.
Postal Orders: Send this form and a check to: AdviceZone, c/o Whitehurst & Clark Fulfillment,
  Raritan Industrial Park, 100 Newfield Avenue, Edison, NJ 08837.

Please send the following books. **I understand that I may return them for a full refund for any reason, no questions asked.**

_____ copies of *Love Advice for Women* at $16.95 each.   _____
Sales tax: Please add 4.5% for products shipped to Virginia addresses.   _____
U.S. priority shipping: $3.50 for first book and $2.00 for each additional book.   _____
International priority shipping: $9.00 for first book and $5.00 for each additional book. _____
                                                                                          Total: $ _____

Name:_____

Address:_____City:_____

State:_____ Zip Code:_____ Country: _____

Telephone:_____ E-mail address:_____

Form of payment:
❏ Check enclosed
❏ Credit Card: ❏ Visa   ❏ MasterCard   ❏ American Express   ❏ Discover

Card number: _____ Expiration date: _____

Name on card:_____ Signature: _____

Please notify me when the following AdviceZone products are available:

❏ *Love Advice for Men*
❏ *Love Advice for Couples*
❏ Love Advice audiotapes
❏ Health, fitness, and nutrition books and audiotapes

Coming Soon to AdviceZone

Love Advice for Men: Everything you wanted to know about love from Austen to Zola

The second book in the *Guide to Love* series gives great love advice to men from classic novels, plays and essays from around the world in an instructive and amusing format. Quotations from the great authors offering classic love advice are mixed with the author's sympathetic musings. Another intriguing element of the AdviceZone series is the interactive nature of the books. Readers can learn more about the love lives of famous authors, communicate with the author, and suggest new quotations at the AdviceZone website.

This is the book that tells men:

- What women really want (Simone de Beauvoir spells it out for you)
- What women really dislike (Jane Austen tells us her pet peeves)
- How to overcome shyness (Shakespeare and Chaucer give you courage)
- How to attract a woman (Stendhal and Ovid have some classic tips)
- How to cure a broken heart (Chaucer helps to ease your pain).

Love Advice for Couples: Everything you wanted to know about love from Austen to Zola

The third book in the *Guide to Love* series concentrates on couples. The quotations and text explain how to find the right mate, how to raise children, how to keep the love alive, along with some of the more difficult issues such as adultery and divorce.

Among other advice, readers can learn:

- Why complementary personalities are best (Plato explains)
- How *not* to pick a spouse (Edith Wharton tells you what you should never do)
- If you should you keep secrets from your partner (Montaigne tells you the best strategy)
- Why you should give your partner some freedom (Chaucer and Tolstoy explain why)
- How to keep love alive (Flaubert gives you a special hint!)